RIPPED BACKSIDES

POSTCARDS FROM BENEATH THE PAVEMENT

RICHARD CABUT

CONTENTS

FOREWORD

Jeff Young

I am reading this book like a detective – poring over secret files discovered in a valise, sifting through a drift archive left behind in the ruins of the city. I imagine someone – let's call him Richard Cabut – has transcribed memory fragments onto a series of index cards, like *Oblique Strategies* for improvising a profile of the protagonist. Some of these fragments resemble xerox photocopies of the soul. Others resemble postcards found in flea markets, cardiograph readouts, voice messages from ghosts on telephone micro-cassettes, Morse Code signals transcribed onto tracing paper...

The materials are volatile. They remind me of nitrate film stock, undeveloped negatives, mixtapes on C60 cassettes, Biro daubs on skinny wrists, unsent love letters to spectral lovers, aphorisms splattered with spilled coffee, napkins smeared with lipstick traces and cigarette burns. I pause between fragments and utter the word 'beauty'. The book inhabits a space between anxiety and uncertainty; its beauty lies in the unstable territory of notebook and dream diary. You might have found a book like this on a bench in a U-Bahn train station in Berlin in the 1980s – or you might find it in a ruined city in the future, in a bookshop that specializes in the underground and the samizdat. It is a document of the subterranean territory of the international drift.

Distortion is important. Temporal fragility. Psychic fallout. To appropriate a passage in the book, perhaps these writings are millions of particles of dust and debris which rush through the most minute cracks, propelled by a dark and overwhelming force. I place the book in my imaginary portable library of the fractured and fragmented: Robert Bresson's *Notes of a Cinematographer*; David Wojnarowicz's *Waterfront Journals*; Murray Bail's *Notebooks*; Franz Fühmann's *Twenty-days: Or Half a Lifetime*; Chris Marker's *La Jetee* and Appollinaire's *Zone*, perhaps? There's a suggestion of Joseph Roth's feuilletons – albeit taken to brevity's edge in a 'whirlwind of codes and signs.' like a Post-

Punk *Arcades Project* or a subterranean Pessoa's trunk. And then the 'London (1978)' sequence reads like the bastard offspring of Joe Brainard's *I Remember* and JG Ballard's *What I Believe*. I believe in people I have known who have disappeared into the eventide like the tiny particulars on a dimmed and washed out negative. And yet the book is distinct unto itself, for these fragments are extracted from Richard's retrieval system of memory, of the almost lost...Memory as cosmos and dust, as séance, as trace element on torn tracing paper.

Occasionally as I was reading the book I wondered if I'd glimpsed Richard Cabut back in the 1980s during my own drift journeys, on autobahns, in cafes and squats, at border crossings, in lowlife bars. We must have sometimes been in the same places, the interzones and debatable territories of drift. Was that Richard I caught a shadow-glimpse of in Bordeaux in that bar on the market square? The flaneur in the military surplus gear reading a paperback in the Kreuzberg squat – was that him? The maladjusted wanderer through European cities – cities haunted by Post-Punk Jan Cremers – is summoned up in these fragments: memories discarded and retrieved like passport pictures found in photo booths, postcards never sent, or notes scrawled on beermats and napkins. This is the beauty of the fractured and fragmented, of memory assembled from the fleeting – when the lost and found is reassembled into a kind of incantation it takes on the quality of magic. Therefore, perhaps these words are spells...

There is a nocturnal atmosphere to the book and the ache of broken dreams, of Brion Gysin's Dream Machine, of the dark – yet beautiful - negative space of spectral void, and that feeling you get sometimes when you wake in the early hours in an unfamiliar city and your mind jolts back to amphetamine midnight – and yet you drag yourself out into the harsh light of daybreak and haul your bones to the convenience store for cigarettes. You walk to your new favourite café, and you hunch over your coffee cup, ripped paper napkin stained with a half-moon, and you begin to sketch your thoughts, where you've been and where you're going to go next. This is my favourite moment in the journey, the vacant, agitated space of anxiety and uncertainty before you pick up your belongings and stride out to the road to tomorrow. *Ripped Backsides* has something of that about it. And it reminds me of listening to the runoff groove of a Lou Reed record and feeling my thoughts accumulate into some kind of approximate, provisional decision to move on... but not until you've finished the cigarette. You listen to the not-quite-silence of the moment. To the delayed inevitable.

You listen to the names of cities – Paris, Warsaw, Krakow, Naples, Berlin! They rattle through your head these demi-monde destinations and potential life or death traps. There is a lull before the beginning of the next lurching journey to the place you need to get to, the defining moment when you realise it's time to move on to the city beyond the horizon where the next event might happen, Years later you write it all down and sift through the Kodaks, the moments coming back to you. An index of transmissions, image drift, signals from the ruins.

Reaching – or overreaching – for a phrase, for a spontaneous response to evoke the spirit of this book I arrived at shrapnel on a moving escalator...Make of that what you will! But there's something about the book and its ruptures and displacements that evokes both collision of fluid movement into the future and the jagged shattering of solidity. *Ripped Backsides* is a scattering of perception and memory shards, a gathering place of moments in a life of improvised motion. Ideally the book should be tattered and mottled with coffee and cognac stains and bookmarked with U-Bahn ticket stubs. Read it in a city that's broken your heart before you move on to the next...

Jeff Young is the author of the Costa Prize shortlisted memoir *Ghost Town: A Liverpool Shadowplay* and *Deliria* published by Rough Trade Books. He's an essayist, scriptwriter for radio and stage and ex TV writer. He collaborates with artists and musicians on installations, sound art, spoken word and performance projects in unusual places. His second memoir *Wild Twin* was published in 2024 by Little Toller.

INTRODUCTION

Richard Cabut

Ripped Backsides is a literary mosaic/montage, an urban travelogue, a creative directory, a hauntological drift, a situationist drift, a fragmentary script (street/interior dialogue), a manual (of cultural myths), city dreamscapes, a form of conceptual lit/art, voodoo poetry (guided hallucinated glimpses into the ether), a series of lists (of aesthetic detail and tightly focused moments and ideas), a wild catalogue of snapshots...

... an ever proliferating network of seductive allusions/illusions, provocative hints, suggestive cross references and connections, a flickering nonlinear flood, a narrative conveyed in surreal jump cuts, a code, a form of short hand...

... a calibrated map... a ruined map.

Take your pick.

Featuring:-

Uncertainties, ambiguities, post-modern instinct, stylised prose, exposés, magical feeling, intractable truths and lies, eulogistic drifts, deliriums, gossip, anti-mythic artistry, absolute affirmations, contemporary classicism, primitive insights, lyrical panic, desolate recounts, luminous intensity, obsessive resonance. Fucked up visions.

These are personal views from beneath the streets, from underneath the pavement – digging through the decaying and/or glittering substrata – peeking into something hidden in the weave of cities I have visited over the years. It's what's there, below the veneer, unknown, that's forever so seductive – the imperceptibles – the book seeks the metaphysical city underneath the temporal one.

This style – trippy, esoteric – is, I feel, the best format with which to explore the more interesting, sometimes provocative and scarily absorbing ideas about our world, and ourselves. It isn't so much a story as an ordering and reordering of emotional and transcendent reverberations.

I've always had a certain favourable disposition towards shuffled tales, follies, shadows glanced in mirrors or windows. The sort of text within allows the language of narration to be poetic – I've taken exact elements and largely stripped them of their specificity – with the aim of lifting the story from the ordinary to the fabled.

Something filmlike, perhaps. At least, an open film that is a liquid thing flowing quickly from one point to another. The film melts into something else, indicating other possibilities beyond whatever the prime situation allows.

Or, an abstract painting. I guess I'm aiming for, in the words of Francis Bacon : '... a sort of moment of magic to coagulate colour and form, so that it gets the equivalent of appearance... in a second you might blink your eyes or turn your head slightly and you look again and the appearance has changed... appearance is... continuously floating.'

Moments of magic.

On these journeys, I took no notes except in my head (apart from the LA/Mexico trip – excerpts from my original 80s road diary are included as an appendix. And the photo on page 41 is of me actually writing that very journal). But the collective thoughts and observations I can personify almost as a spirit accomplice following me around wherever I went. And this book is a form of automatic writing – driven by and to the spirits – an album of rhetorical missives which I never sent home at the time.

I was looking intensely but always from a certain remove, giving leeway to insight and simultaneously decelerating the creative process by delaying the reaction till now. Back then, I found myself in the next uncertain place, sampling the culture and spacing it back now in scramble segments. I was and still am looking for the strange beauty that I touch when coming into a town for the first time – the discoveries and connections that suddenly appear.

The plot of the book is a poem. I look for the image that gives rise to impulse and impetus. I'm excited by realisation and revelation not unessential logic and certitude or... the solid. If a poem, if a city – if the poetic line in the city – doesn't astonish or provoke just a little by the image it throws up it's a flop. The poetic line resounds with a tension where inner and exterior converge – on the curve between the image and awareness of it. Is this a form of transcendence? Maybe.

I agree that all verities over a certain period grow into the vaunted 'fiction about the self'. In that respect this is a continuous autobiography of ideas: like a three dimensional grid. A map of a thought process, the very act of describing, which is confessional.

I'm on a quest to find the psyche of the city – swirls with glimpsed faces, found materials, geometric literary shapes. A stream of sparks. Evening alchemy, fissures and rifts where cities lose their hold – existentialist dreams that are a metaphor for ...

... my own bearings, perhaps. A display of self-excavation – psychic archaeology, if you like. Digging through the city strata, simply to, in the end, find the fullness of my own freaky soul, to find that area – where the world in here meets the world out there –

where the authentic state is to be established. And concepts like destiny or future can be considered.

Says German-American political theorist Hannah Arendt (1906-75), as related in the *Philonomist*: 'The impossible quest for oneself can only be fulfilled in the act of narration.'

I think I understand why she says 'impossible' – because, really, all these journeys, and the telling of them, are a quest to find oneself and to disappear at the same time. Half the time, when we're looking at ourselves deeply, we're looking for someone who doesn't want to be found. And that act of narration is fulfilling because it frees us from the very stories we are telling.

Relating our stories is, in the end, an attempt to grow or move beyond them. 'We tell ourselves stories in order to live,' said Joan Didion – I'd add that: we tell ourselves stories in order to find and then alter ourselves, which may very well add up to the same thing in the end.

For Laura Board – my fellow traveller

Singin' la la la la la la la la
La la la la la la la la
La la la la la la la la la
– Iggy Pop, *The Passenger, 1977.*

The form of the city changes faster, alas, than the
human heart
– Raymond Queneau, 1967.

Man passes there through forests of symbols
Which look at him with understanding eyes
– Charles Baudelaire, *Flowers of Evil*, 1857.

We are not in the least afraid of ruins... We carry a
new world here, in our hearts. That world is growing
in this minute – Buenaventura Durruti, 1936.

David Locke : Wouldn't it be better if we could just
forget old places. Forget everything that happens.
Just throw it all away, day by day.
Robertson, the Dead Man: Unfortunately, the world
doesn't work that way.
David Locke : But, it doesn't work the other way
either – and that's the problem
- Michelangelo Antonioni, *The Passenger*, 1975.

We are bored in the city, there's no longer any
Temple of the Sun. Between the legs of the women
walking by, the Dadaists imagined a monkey wrench
and the surrealists a crystal cup. That's lost... We are
bored in the city
– Ivan Chtcheglov, *Formulary for a New Urbanism*,
1953.

Memory is redundant: it repeats signs so that the
city can begin to exist
– Kathy Acker, private email to McKenzie Wark,
1996, quoted in *After Kathy Acker*, Kris Kraus, 2017.

Nowhere/Boredom.
For weeks afterwards, I wasn't sure if I was back.

AMSTERDAM (1984)

Magic bus from Victoria/Reading A. Crowley's Magic
Record of the Beast 666 –
*John Symonds (Editor), Kenneth Grant (Editor)/
Euro sub cult survivors trashed on the streets /Small
festival in a squatted farmhouse, a walk away from the
centre/Euro festival travellers sleep in a giant loft in the
barn, overhead hundreds of dope plants dry out, leaves
fluttering onto and into people's empty sleeping bags
in the morning – bonne chance at the border/ Plume,
a Camden bohemian, from the band Dog Star, plays
saxophone in the lane outside the farmhouse. Like
an illustrative scene from the Beat Generation/Most
residents hate the dope culture/Twisted nerves.*

Dazed city made from a hypnotic loop. The city lives
in a hypnogogic coil.

Girl in squatted barn, across the canal, down the road,
shrieks. Mouth open like Bacon.

People refuse to turn wretched refusal into style.
Trashed aesthetic.

Dialogue: It's an observation on the waning of
youthful dreams, isn't it?

German skinheads on the street. The make-up of
events, illustrating non sense.

Dialogue: Madeline was shocked for a moment when
her parents became Zen Buddhist priests.

Everyone listens to low event horizon music.

Dialogue: ... An anorexic psych-out... I was... I am...

People say: If I'm not touched it is impossible to
sleep. I never sleep.

Vulnerability – like some philosophy at some other remove. Vulnerability on the street feeds back on itself.

On the street: Addictions and tantrums. As though your life depended on it.

Out of boredom of despair, out of despair of boredom. Predictable affronts of bohemia.

People without a hometown. All things are (under) valued for their instability.

Sex: She has a chased and unsullied soul.

I am: Dehydrated lights and distance – wavelength blue underlined. Teenage heart gone molten.

Disorderly magic. There are only so many times you can watch the same sorcery and find it beguiling. *Forever*.

Enlarged to epic scale only by some weird neuroscience. No access to profound love.

People in bars are soft and childlike but remain informed. Like paranoid characters in film in slow motion, scored by Miles Davis in '73.

People look for an ongoing interaction with art away from any reality principle.

People read Malraux at the tram stop for secrets of human soul. Spoiler – people are even more unhappy than anyone thinks.

Question on people's minds: Does the city give or take even the smallest amount of transcendence to or from the world?

Defined by negatives. Everything seems like an affirmation. The big question: What do you despise most?

Outside reality – almost inhumanly perfect. Awake dreams of desire. Impenetrable city seduced.

Buildings dissolve: An architecture designed around yearning.

Unseen forces, currents of sexual tension. Thick.

No capacity for self-analysis. For the time being.

Sex: Dusty room. A haze – conscious distance from yourself.

Passer-by defaults to literature. What is the attraction of existentialism?

Jan Cremer sleeps in a graveyard of abstract pictures.

People's faces are readable. But not as a sequence of facts.

Dusk with sparks, ghosts sitting in seats, instant nostalgia, street-level mysticism.

There is a split between impulse and *impulse.*

The rain flows eternally. Like King Lear creating the storm for self.

Convolutions that come out of a richer imagination. Familiar dualism.

Dialogue: I think it was panic that drove me from one to another. One to the other.

Man sits alone in cemetery. No moments for high winter clouds of resistance. But also the trees.

Let's have a medieval body and soul allegory.

Walter Benjamin's image is *detached from aura by mechanical reproduction*. But what about dramatic tension?

Sex: A finger touches naked foot. Channelling.

She forgets her suicide plans. We never talk about dramatic tension, she says, tragically.

Dam Square: People think other people are only interested in neat arrangement of reversals.

The city heard though an open window: The repetition of a dance melody, an ordinary waltz, 16-bar sequence composed of two 8-bar parts, characterized by the regular inclusion of a pause… which might just echo for ever.

People look at porn magazines as an exploration of consciousness. Sexual meditation: Room with a view.

Dialogue: He would fuck a lot better if he imagined that he was acting in a movie. A bad movie.

People experience various ailments. Balance of elements.

The ordering of parts that inverts a previous ordering. Expressionist version of *The Birthday Party*. That's entertainment.

Dialogue: I've been so sickeningly poor all my life.

Inner psychic click that signifies peace. Magnitude of role.

Inner conflict that has tragic potential.

Dialogue: '*Oh you weak, beautiful people who simply give up...*'

The dramatic understanding that one moment of revelation (even one relentlessly awful) can replace dialogue.

People's lives are always based on other people's lives. Mainly Marguerite Duras, Elio Vittorini and Bertolt Brecht, Also, Arnold Schoenberg and Wassily Kandinsky. Take your pick.

The catastrophe of personality. Speck in the eye for the self.

It's all food, sex and vanity – accumulated imaginatively: Identification.

Hotel. Hypnotic energy. Until hands stop shaking.

Interior. Claustrophobic. Narrative style: Both voiceover and flashback.

Writer as detective looking for clues. Subjective camera involves reader in radical voyeurism. Fashion for technique – writer as detective never seen on page or screen. Point of view is that of audience. Clues to what?

A tale told by an idiot. Never tells what it is, only what it is like.

Unsatisfying return to ordinary life. Most are drawn to the *sic transit* theme.

People masturbating to texts of revolutionary politics. The money shot is Hollywood redemption.

Dominant mood: Creative introspection. No easy characterisations to adhere to. Motif of destiny as a counter flow.

People are very sad that cosy poetic pre-60s realism has given way to anxious ill at ease disdainfulness of the New Wave.

Funeral rites, freaky dancing, lost decades, ongoing moments and altered states.

Passers-by are mainly between lives. Everyone knows what is being expressed – nothing is communicated.

Dialogue: Godard says the real problem is to *get back to zero* – agreed?

Archetypal city look... of curiosity which comes over people's faces when nothing much happens. Constantly.

Image of Polyester. Lights go down, like the physical ache in people's demeanour.

Anyway, there's no real cinema, she said.

Anyway, it's not a real book, he said.

From a sourcebook for the contemporary collective
subconscious. A sudden shifting of scene.

Moi, je. Realism: Genuine spectacle.

BARCELONA, VALENCIA and MADRID
(1968, 2004 and several assorted years over the 1980s, 1990s and 2000s)

Man breasts on beach, plus hair/Fear of the sea until the last day; too late/Exotic taste of crème caramel pudding/Souvenirs: castanets, sombrero, drum/Parents' applaudable refusal to attend bull fight/My fortune is told by gypsy tarot reader in Parque del Retiro, Madrid – I will be rich, of course/40 degrees in the shade/FC Barcelona and 100,000 approx. capacity Camp Nou/ Messi, Neymar and Suarez/Ciutat Vella (Old Town) – the gangs plan next move/Sagrada Família by Antoni Gaudí (1852–1926) – a paean to unfinished business/ The devil's work in Benedictine abbey, Santa Maria de Montserrat.

Flaming image. What you need you haven't found.

Gracia: Revved right up to the point where the unruly starts to seep into the dizzy.

Swirling up tempo pacing. Curvy and searing, sweet. Insouciance can't quite mask a fastidious construction.

There is no lost time. Prone to graphic internal dialogues, booze hardened.

Art and symmetry provide respite. But just for a short while. *Scratch in the sand, won't let go his hand.*

Dialogue: I am a poetess who hasn't found her real voice yet – what's *essential* is that I give up my life to verse utterly. It's the least I can do. Of course, of course.

In the sky. Objects representing something I can't understand. The importance of looking up and down.

Woman reads Klaus Theweleit's two volumes of *Male Fantasies*, now recognized as a pre-eminent work on the body, war and fascism. She says he likes horror stories.

People say quoting some book they have read on the bus: 'I never get nowhere but I pay my own fare all the way.' Better to just walk, then, perhaps.

City as movie. The belief in director to choose from the maelstrom of *everything* only those details that comprise certain significance. Do people buy into those meanings?

The everlasting question: What is my desire?

Passers-by walk to find the ecstasy of some idea of wilderness. Slowly.

Man only has sex in front of mirror – for obvious reasons. Carnival looking glass. Skin reflects.

Sad stories told in bar. Psychic violence extends through time

Sex: Nobody knows about life who hasn't breathed the air she had breathed in and out, she imagines.

Light-headed ambiguity or just a flow? Emetic either way. Smooth going down though.

Art happens in high heel shoes. Senselessly. Fassbinder is aware.

People wonder if they would rather be characters in a film, or in a book or in a bad poem?

Thoughts of passers-by include: Language of clothes, structure, ceremony of wardrobe and other ways of heaven.

Passer-by trips and displaces all destination – thinks time is probably devoid of objects.

She doesn't care that the city doesn't care that she exists. City is disappointed. City starts to construct victim narrative in response.

Conceptual would-be architectural projects in dim past – 'classic-dreamlike' – unearthly research into various individuals in up-to-minute society.

Pickpockets say making films doesn't make you an artist, but *living the life* of an auteur does.

Pickpocket advises: Artist – draw crime scenes: steal hearts. Including my own.

The street: Self-perpetuating narrative that refreshes itself without the need for climax or resolution. A good trick.

Passer-by daydreams about the recollection of the smell of longing and impulse. Hell.

Sex: Her rhythm changes the order of the world, he thinks.

Dialogue: I don't like speaking in riddles. Or poetic verse. Same difference.

Dialogue: He's going to be in big trouble if he doesn't find the magic again.

People in the best sunglasses talk about psychological repercussions that visual disengagement has on the psyche. Like they are always on the verge of something, they say.

In a bar woman misremembers something she may

have read somewhere or other – *the image is landlord of illusion. Memory is the tenant* – or, she wonders, *have I just made that up?*

Passers-by perceivable only by the gravity they exert.

Artificial things are better than fake things say people who spend their money in neon lit alleys. Corporate shamanism.

City defined by the actions it observes, and has observed, as much as by anything else – including borders or architecture.

Fear of sensual disorder. Tzara, Richter, Ball, Duchamp, Breton.

Dialogue: *Just so.*

Everywhere: Litany of micro-satire and irony. Relevant only to committed absurdists.

People hire interior designers to create mood of neurasthenia. A-Z of madness.

Dark matter. Porn film without the money shot. No ending of beginning of the ending – level of boredom upped substantially.

Dialogue: I really feel that I can attract the city to me by being the person I will become.

Hatred of atmosphere created by intense dreams. There's nothing they won't do to you.

Mayhem of resplendence of material goods. Smell of burning beautiful things.

People reject the romantic expressionist approach in favour of the matter of fact. Collective dreaming.

People listen through the thin walls to hear the emanations of other people's lives. What is that sound? What is this one?

Dialogue: I dote on him. He is blind to any red lines – all geniuses are.

The air feels like... S & M. Body politic as metaphor.

Extraordinary bliss – involvement as a matter of fact. Animal.

Narrative devices that seduce in locked rooms.

People read Keats about those who pass into nothingness ...

There is a passage of time – maybe ten seconds. More?

BERLIN (1987)

Transit van trip to play a few gigs/Temperature approaching -20 degrees/Van spins 360 degrees on iced-over autobahn – near death feeling, car behind veers off road and down a steep grass bank. We stop to make sure they're OK. We then slip and slide on down the road/Inadvertent smuggling of amphetamine sulphate across the heavy manners Cold War border, forgotten in zip pocket of folded and packed leather trousers – they search everywhere but there/So cold that the city traffic stops for a while – the silence is stunning/We stay at the ultra-organised KOB squat, with its own dorms, bar, cinema, concert hall – amazing – better than council housing and some private sector housing in the UK/ Utter alcoholic degradation – guitarist finishes his thousandth beer, vomits immediately into his glass, and then drinks that down... to the dregs/Wasters and drifters from the hinterlands/Eating chocolate spread and black bread in the well-equipped kitchen/I play bass a micro- beat out of time like a mis-firing heart beat/Nerves/Junk shops selling Nazi memorabilia/ Tube trains passing through abandoned stations left un-opened since the war, complete with station names written in distinctive Fraktur typeface/Returning to the squat in the morning after a heavy night out, as usual – the look of contempt and hatred in the eyes of 9-5 commuters.

Until zero remains along freezing strasse, where nothing can alight again.

Last gasp of past. A wall of words. Or vice versa.

Night town of seediness and integrated circuits, fever steam drifting over forever frost.

Abstraction at its most suggestive. Concentrated insanity that animates dislocated atmosphere and charms into (man-made) adrenaline.

Narcissistic dream state removed from everything, except the *lustprinzip*. Sacrifice to gratification is itself a pleasure, in principle.

Man in bar orders last sacrament. Toasts future already dead.

City listens to urban soundtrack by Tangerine Dream. But prefers ambient incidental fuzz. Listening to the future filter through.

Stray people meander in pearl-grey haze of world; unmeasured street, and cars that die in the bitterness.

Ashen face beneath the wall, still breathing cold steam, digging into dreams that no one wants to escape from.

Humming of light industry speaks in symbols. Economy of thought.

Sex: Heightened by loneliness and exile. Mad. Cold sheets better than cold streets.

Art gallery: People speak in left-wing outrage quotation marks in voice of Orson Welles and Sid Vicious.

People in the Kreuzberg squats read aloud from book: *I can get in more trouble in two days of not trying then most people can get into in a lifetime of trying really hard.*

Dialogue: I wanted to start hating Brecht but instead I started to hate myself.

Have night and fog really lifted? Electronic cluster. Base rhythm. Like info not meant for us.

Areas in any city to head for: The port of saints, low standard football grounds, mystic cathedrals, gates of heaven, the Wall, avenues of ecstatic truth, fabricated places of poetic fact, wasteland of mirrors, forgotten places, libraries which stock books by Kafka.

Avoid at all costs: Temporary autonomous zones.

Shadow images on curtain walls of city set. They are part of what is at stake. Badlands.

The sky and moon melt. Adorno and Horkheimer look on. But don't care.

Schöneberg. Map is full of inconsistencies. Nothing left to locate. That is that.

Passer-by smokes one cigarette after the other, leaves behind traces of smoke in the air. Smoke gets in city's eye. City follows passer-by street to street.

Concept intensifies to a tone, becoming emotion. A process of dynamics.

The tune never mediates without an image. Imagination is the vernacular of the song. Of the soul, some say.

Passer-by whistles a tune. Terence Stamp in Pasolini's *Theorem*. Confusing the disposition of the world.

Dialogue: Memories are only worthwhile if connected to consequence or product – I don't remember which. Do you?

Dialogue: The only body I'll belong to is one that doesn't exist.

Top of deserted hilltop park, street lights flash code; yellow – the only visible warm smears of and on the city. Lights gently drag viewer out of dim urban labyrinth.

Homesickness for dying forms that inhabit algebra of the city. It doesn't add up.

Fantastic crooked angles. Wide-angle camera contorts physiognomy and geometry. Noir. A view that filters best through heavy cigarette smoke.

Needed: A motif to represent the ordinary commuter's instability and descent into underworld.

We inhabit the *Trümmerfilm*, or the rubble aesthetic. Remake and rerun.

Sheen of sweat in German winter. Full on provocation. Pull on provocation… like a mask.

The end of politics and the impossibility of utopia – everyone says it makes sense.

Dialogue: Strange I feel so numb when I should be feeling the most horrendous loss – the loss of friends and the loss of self. Multiplied a hundred fold.

The sound of a several pianos playing slightly different tunes in downstairs bar. Husky voices. Fumes of Becks and Sekt. Highly toxic.

Everyone in the squats is waiting for the heavy touch. Gossiping into their pillows, meanwhile.

Man in fleapit of his fantasy is open wide to the marvellous at the perimeters of his imagination. There is nothing on the other side of this, he feels.

Looking for isolated and finer feeling/s behind the tracking. Street as phantasmagoria. It's a secret.

Sex: Surprise at quality of anxiety, swollen.

The streets lie in the shadows – fantastic perspective on distortions. Dreamy.

Dialogue: I'm looking for the vanished lights. And I'm at the vanishing point.

The moon beams. A viewpoint of vested interest. Magician, meanwhile, feels tricked by physics.

Agreed: Redemptive endings are sophistic and unalluring. Devotion to the future remains pure.

New vision: The city, like some Warhol movies, is watched several frames per second more slowly than the speed at which it was shot.

The city's drama is undercut by deadpan narrative. Temporal like distance strategy.

The art of reflection. Not many truly believe that others exist.

On the corner: Emphatic truths, absolute moments.

Woman in bar says mood of city is stylised, analysed repetition. And bad luck rumours. Bad luck for *you*.

Interior dialogue: *Things I like* – work boots, surplus military trapper caps, snow in the park, silent films, Fender Precision bass guitar (cream/white, made in 1977, same as Sid Vicious'. Sold years later for a pittance, for no real reason), silent nights, the idea of the atomic city, small bottles of spirits from newspaper kiosks outside the U-Bahn, old smelly books, playing in a band live – audience as co-author etc, Kreuzberg hangouts/clubs, speed, brutality chic, endless German cigarettes (American blend), Expressionism, purgation – the process of spiritual

purification of souls in purgatory, traction between
quiet pragmatism and terminal degradation, bleak
poetry of modern urban eroticism (in Kreuzberg,
again), poisoned cake at midnight, porno messages
from beyond, no TV anywhere.
Things I dislike: German sausages/any meat (or
fish), barking dogs, beards, well-rounded people,
modernist myth of the artist, people sleeping six or
eight to a room, reduction of Eros to power, punk,
the strict avoidance of loss of emotional control, total
organisation.

Dialogue: Some cities like scrutiny only on occasion.
Some cities like their secrets to remain hidden.

Write. A diary of the probable and improbable.

People grow boldly in an atmosphere of staleness, and
stale air.

Post-modern cross overs. The voyeur's profound collaboration with the exhibitionist.

LONDON (1978-present)

I believe in 'What I Believe' *by JG Ballard published in* Interzone, *#8, Summer 1984. A prose poem. Originally published in French in* Science Fiction *#1 (ed. Daniel Riche) in January 1984.*

I believe in abolishing time and having music always, in order to burn boxes, invoke and provoke disorderly magic and remove rust.

I believe in not believing in the disbelief of terminal nostalgia, in being tired all the time and in writing best when I weep or sleep.

I believe in the lowest application of the authentic, and those levels on the farther side of aesthetics, and in eating unpalatable truths for breakfast, with salt.

I believe in the message of fairy tales, in the endless road, in over fed fantasies and flat lies, and in the litany of missed chances and glances.

I believe in the beautiful universe created by the allure of Kate and Megan.

I believe in anything said by voices resonant of the mid-20th century. Smokers' voices – Silk Cut, Embassy or Benson and Hedges.

I believe in people I have known who have disappeared into the eventide like the tiny particulars on a dimmed and washed out negative.

I believe that life is based on an innumerable number of illusions – some of them – mostly the masochistic ones – are about ourselves.

I believe in people who adopt a reckless gait in the face of a sadistic random universe, the smell and texture of which is greasy gin and grubby lino.

I believe in anything that drones on nihilistically, in thwarted love, and in minds reeling with amazement.

I believe in the vague and stupid somewhere or other between the elation of chance and the enigma of failure and calamity.

I believe in an epic dream about a house being hit by a tornado, in slow motion, with millions of particles of dust and debris which rush through the most minute cracks, propelled by a dark and overwhelming force.

I believe in violent shadows, in the savagely lyrical, in anonymity from which we all came from, in black cats that have been hit by cars.

I believe in the smell of boredom, the howl of people smiling for no discernible reason, in the inability to grasp my dreams last night because the child inside was crying and keeping me awake.

I believe in familiars which become acquaintances, almost friends, in characters drifting, waiting to be touched, in those with eyes ablaze with exquisite feelings they do not wish to share with anyone, in the idea of perishing in the wailing infinities.

I believe in men and women of tough luck and no chances, and in saddened reclusive heroes of the 21st century, and in unkempt charlatans, too.

I believe in Jan Cremer and Jack Kerouac and Zbigniew Cybulski and Marek Hlasko and their bohemian adventures, and in artists whose minds have been honed and jolted almost clairvoyant by psychological maladjustment, who personify all the sorrows and contrition of the city.

I believe in everything.

I believe in an ineffable something, a little mouse with clogs on, in the holy moment of looking in the mirror, in God in the cinema of his dreams.

I believe in unalterable reality not just as a hook but as a starting point for a narrative that continues to unfold to reveal fresh sources of amazement.

I believe in getting back to natural fibres and earthy colours, in depraved amorality and in an endless cycle of futile revolt.

I believe in stopping once and a while and saying 'No, that is not me', in going nowhere, in whistling a tune of orgasmic grievance and complaint all way.

I believe in transformative sorcery, internal aftershave and four tarot readings per day to maximise confusion and increase psychic fallout.

I believe in shadowy things at the edge of your vision, in the gaudiness and confidence to dream of those fabulous things, so tumbled and important that we're all still all trying to work them out even now.

I believe in apathy and delirium, in being possessed by the glittering jazz of angels between the lines, in less than zero.

I believe that nothing is unfading enough not to believe in, including walking on a tightrope, and a whirlwind of codes and signs.

I believe in spiritual disintegration, in Baudrillard's sunglasses in the bath, in chocolates for breakfast all the time, in boredom of cultural artefacts.

I believe in rampant ambition, in books that start with

people who are afraid to merge on freeways in Los Angeles, in remorseless greed, and self-improvement.

I believe in attention span culture, soulless necro academia, in being born modern, in the power and glory of the leisure industry.

I believe in having hair swept backwards and aloft as if caught in a sudden gust, in looking for a kiss, in *Looking for a Kiss*, in magnetic clarity, in Bresson.

I believe in the eye meeting the light, in bruises borne of banality, in disgorging the psychological underworld writhing just beneath our collective human hum.

I believe in everything immeasurable and out of bounds, in *Disorderly Magic and Other Disturbances* , in my psychic mother and in some additional visions and visitations.

I believe in the Black Madonna, Queen of Poland, in alchemists who think matter in any form is, in some way or other, a living thing, in Charles Baudelaire and Samuel Beckett, in generational trauma, in the self as value-added nothingness, in the idea of the poetic truth – one which grasps, like barbed wire, the essence of truth, in the foggy notion of spiritual precociousness as a brash and audacious refusal to give in to the state of the world or the universal situation, in psychic pre-ordering of an easier life, in a blind universe running amok, in the poetic self-metamorphized through artistry, in postcards to nowhere and in blank spaces.

I believe in the ghost of Frederick Chopin's piano, in the ghost of a chance, in the bedroom as landscape, in my deepest unknown desires, in pointless detours, in never sleeping enough and always feeling like you are standing on the edge of a precipice, in cheap things, in Roy Lichtenstein's word 'Whoom' (because it rhymes with womb), in the audacity of lists, in the Fall (not the band), in Federico Fellini, in the inevitable victory of Bugs Bunny, in obscene books, in kipper ties, in the Twist, in Bryon Gysin's assertion that: *no, poets don't own words*, in the neo-primitive, in the question: will you still love me tomorrow?, in the death of Warhol and some others, in the absolute virility of Harry and William, in the excess of belief, the sheer excess of belief.

I believe in Harold Pinter, in Krzysztof Penderecki, in the good idea someone or other had that the desire to pray is already prayer, in the quality of miracles, in not believing in myself, in getting paid for every move I make, in being in the Zone forever, in escaping the Zone, in the dark end of the street, in getting on the bus and not off the bus, in the light on the tip of the snake's tongue, that the glass on the table moves on its own, in petulant straining after figurative and allegorical meaning, in shopping for art, expensive watches and drugs, in manifestations of consolation for the misery of the chimera of real life in the spectacular society, in the frost covered grass and the soot of hell, in 70s hi-fi systems, in the word 'fuck', in the salt in human bodies, in Francois Truffaut, in photographs of the earth from the moon, in all conspiracy theories, in liars everywhere, in saying 'Sh-boom' (because it rhymes with 'Whoom'), in *Guernica* and *Nausea*, in belief as an authentic experience.

I believe in my psychotherapist, in anyone and everyone who believes in me, in the invention of the ballpoint pen, in being in a dancing mood, in electronic speech synthesisers mimicking the human voice, in space as a stream – it's surface onyx, in David Wojnarowicz and Nat Finkelstein, in the future as the glare in a clear and brilliant sky, in the limits of unlimited individuality, in plumbing the depth of the ocean and the height of the sky, in Friedrich Nietzsche's 'luminous concreteness' – what you see ain't what you get, in mute things and louvred ceilings, in JG Ballard's fear 'that everything has happened; nothing exciting or new or interesting is ever going to happen again ... the future is just going to be a vast, conforming suburb of the soul,' in the very belief in the soul, and in the dawn annihilated by love and hate, in the disturbance in the visual, mental and spiritual fabric allowing for the emergence of this writing, in the withdrawal from the 'sphere of wishes'.

I believe in London, and Dunstable and Luton and Sutkowczyzna and Jaslowiecka, in stolen land and stolen kisses, in looking again and again until the same image changes into something else entirely, in bringing the world to a standstill, in unnatural light concealing/blurring materiality, in an easy glide to a true ambit, in waiting for enthusiasm to return, in never waiting for the enthusiasm to return, in dissatisfaction as a value, in Godard's remark that tracking shots are a question of ethics, I believe in life as a tracking shot.

I believe in direct encounters with being let down – cities are meant to let you down, it's for the best – a disruption of our perception that they are more, or less, than we consider or want them to be.

I believe in making the world via geometry and hanging out with the Bacchic mob, in tiny characters assuming epic proportions in a bigger picture (framed and hung), in perturbing implications.

I believe that the city is a dark negative to the claim of somewhere else, not here, in the thought that there's never enough moonlight out there, and that gravity will drag weights and movements into words.

I believe that the city speaks a weird language which

we would do well to learn, that the flow of space in the city is a confusion of model with reality – the map and the territory, that the city is the snake's camouflaged coil.

I believe in level surfaces, in the point where language does not matter yet, in a picture's quietness, in the hidden answer to all mysteries, in the place where revelation has occurred, in liquid thought as firm as glass, in the term *art for art's sake*, in the smell of certain words and sounds, in the difference engine, in Lou Reed's idea that electricity comes from other planets, in unity and separate existence, in a landscape of hard details and bafflement, in the meaningful announcement of the time of day, in trajectory of drama, in smooth coloured glass in shallow water, in journeys to the centre of the earth, in the indisputable idea that art (including poetry, lists and cities) is whatever you say it is.

I believe in the nude ascending and descending and falling down a staircase, in going back to cities to see how I've changed, in the margins between people, in dissipation as part of meaning, in the very best clothes, boutiques and perfumeries.

I believe in a world of marketing catchwords and publicity mottos, in common or garden blackness and illumination, in the *pfttt* of nothing at all, in existing in many different sequences of events at the same time, in the moment when you realise you are there.

I believe in the colours black and orange, but not wholly in blue, or grey, in the rough current of the river as it swirls past the dead body, in being held captive, in cities whose parts do not fit into each other, in pictures of the depths as abstract art, in stopping at the sight and thought of the city, in everything we touch turning into appearance. And disappearance.

The angle from which emotions are not authentic.

LOS ANGELES (1987)

*Please refer to Appendix 2 for excerpts from my original
and authentic Los Angeles diary.*

For sale, charm of desire – to take us fully unawares.
Chink beyond the material. Once removed.

Sex: Kiss me with your celebrity mouth – at times
when even a sado-masochist must shout out loud.

Sex: Until nothing is left on stained sheets except
maybe some gift to catch fire again.

Sex: Kiss me with your celebrity mouth while it is
right to dig deep dreams.

Sensation of life kicking at heels to just move.
Hurrying to a place where angels
fear to dive.

A holy void swinging with dreams of coming. Is
wonder enough?

A range of cultural abstractions. Locating its own
texture. Kiss me.

T-shirt slogan on the street: There is zero moral
upshot.

Top questions people asks themselves everyday:-

How many people are you?
Only twenty years till doomsday?
Are we entering the new space age?
Is there a paranormal method of protest?
Can prophesies save us from ourselves?

For the devotionally intangible everything is fiction.
A fashionable critical commonplace, yes?

Life is photography, death is cinema – Susan Sontag upside down, spinning over and over, once more, in her grave.

Path to salvation via tattered pop trash clues. Simplification of contact with outside world.

Man on corner thinks about making film about false consciousness and the culture industry. And emotionless Hollywood actor reappraises his life.

Passer-by mesmerised by faculty to compress space and fold feelings in calibrated imagination.

Quick thoughts: Walking on nicotine egg shells/ Medicated/Enslaved to vibrations/ Conjuring magic because I can/Charmed by a beauty that no one else can see, only me, I think/Atonal static everywhere.

Young woman in café drinks coffee as though waiting for her close-up. Imagines her swelling self. Bursting.

The resolution always comes via the close-up reveal.

Hanging out in the galleries with social monsters. Monsters talk, but not at length, about Robert Rauschenberg, Joseph Beuys, Frank Stella, Jim Dine, Richard Serra, Sol LeWitt, Claes Oldenburg, Bruce Nauman, Joan Miró, David Hockney, Ellsworth Kelly, Francesco Clemente, Susan Rothenberg, Cinderella, Poison, Whitesnake, Motley Crue, Def Leppard, U2 and Michael Jackson.

I buy secret notebook in which to write stray words of the unloved. And to catalogue grave erotic concerns.

Holding on to the night. Imaginary life styles. Retreat into the typical. All at once.

People tune in to encrypted sounds and accelerated motion. They wear dark glasses. So do I.

People feeling deep nostalgia for psychic world of lipstick traces.

Sex: Obscure confined sound from TV in corner. (Unseen) *The Tonight Show Starring Johnny Carson.* He says (maybe/not): Every sexual situation is an overdramatic paraphrase of an incomplete transaction.

TV: Movement towards something constantly missing. Lack. Bad luck.

Image of a woman alone at café writing. Ghetto theory or cultural studies.

I realise what I want to be. A cautionary tale.

Dialogue: Most people I know don't have private lives they have walk on parts – not even lead roles – in the lives they act in.

Sex: Slow insertions – plans, meanwhile, for leisurely amorphous future.

Dialogue: I am not scared of America but it absolutely frightens the life and death out of me.

Spiritual emergencies and pre-existing conditions. Cruising for cruising's sake.

Mythology of people that I admire – essential loneliness.

AA – Anorexia and Aloneness. Everything is fabulous.

Philosophy of art – stupefying erotic-morbid

hallucinations.

People are encouraged to sit silently on the peak of old sad dreams.

People use the word 'reflexive' with genuine feeling.

People on Sunset use the word 'hyperreal'. There is no other option, they feel.

People in Venice are definitely shadow souls in glare of sun. Hot.

Everyone thinks in snapshots. Click. Pure reflection.

LA: Depths of spirituality. Religious abstraction of compulsive repetition.

Mindset of post-modernity. Ruin in every sphere. No matter.

Days and nights of mild invocation projected across empty space.

Lives at uncertain pace. Delirium has value meaning.

Woman in bar says: Best sex is five of cups. Other woman says: No, it is the queen of wands. *Just like in that film.*

People think at the speed of the screenplay. Thoughts and pace multiplied by mixing signals.

Subject confounds his own mood – wonders about signifiers of private engagement and marks of dirty fingers and hands. This adds texture.

Sex: She puts her hand on lower back, talks about secrets that might need to be revealed.

Ritual acts. The secret sound of the city is the buzz of a TV malfunction.

Downtown: 15 per cent of people contemplate the metaphysical definitions of freedom 8 per cent of the time.

My secret is a dry whisper of nowhere.

California: Something beautifully oozing from the inside.

People look for tiny buried compensation of technology. A junkyard dreaming.

Favourite perfume (on Melrose): Death of Romance.

People would rather be in cartoons than pornos. And sitcoms without with or without laugh track. It doesn't matter.

Empty air is filled with anxious words. Psychoanalysis as metaphor for critique.

Dialogue: I tried to talk back to somebody on TV. I couldn't get a word in edgeways.

Dialogue: How can I easily turn my emotions into product? Are you *feeling* it?

People on Venice Pier are the last people on earth.

Robert Bresson behind the camera. He thinks of 24-hour room service.

Importance of irony in a universe of confirmation.

Signs. Euphemism as direction misinformation. Going down?

The city sings at a certain pitch: A hush that can be held onto.

Commodity and spectacle: Inaccessible isolation and vast unthinkable existence. Two for the price of one.

Life in the hills: Stale weed and uptight stars, disorientated. Teetering. Fun. No fun.

Soundtrack: Wasteland music (music that sounds like heightened exhaustion in outermost margins). Live Evil.

Teenage runaways in black leather jackets – Modernist venture to propel classical past. The semiologist as artist.

Dialogue: I'm not a villain. I'm a hero. But in a different movie. You know?

Stillness is no longer stillness.

People never go out or do anything – the live at deathly pace – because Jean Baudrillard said 'Speed is out!', and 'all trips have already taken place.' People cannot project any more.

Halo of memory replaced by new associations. Everything has been consummated.

Nothing is direct; how did I get here? Follow the signs.

I am in thrall to negation – unavailable authenticity adds to cool.

The city skyline is always sad. Like start of finish of low budget documentary. Inanimate.

T-shirt slogan on the street: Narcotic sedative

tranquillizer depressant
sleeping pill soporific anaesthetic painkiller analgesic anodyne barbiturate bromide morphine opium laudanum calmative Pethidine Nembutal Glutethimide.

Dialogue: Everything is still there, but it will no longer come to life.

LA mood: Anhedonia (happiness is merely a fleeting diversion from overwhelming lament).

Mythological events:-

Microwaves
Sunscreen
Sunglasses
Pharmaceutical drugs
Headphones
Eating while angry
Sex while fragmented
Artificial blue light
Nylon clothing
Antibiotics
Sleeping pills

Passer-by fleeing from and towards faltered states –
while looking for the grand gesture, with an eye on
the tracking shot into horizon.

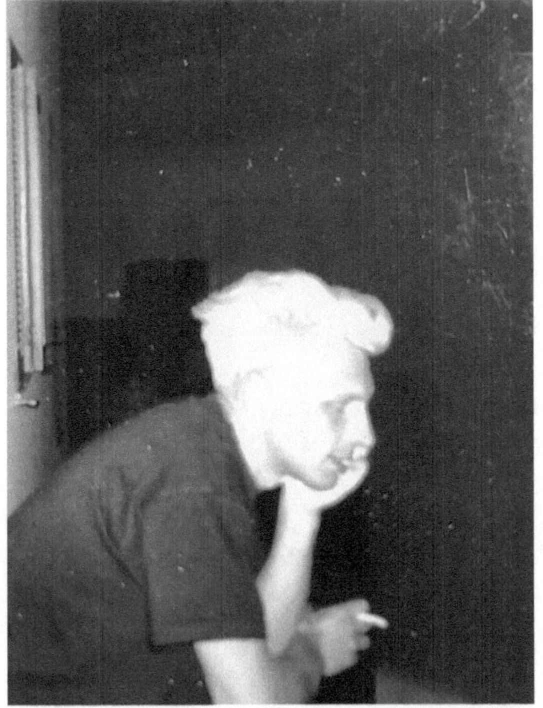

An interchangeable scene occurs. What makes you afraid?

MANCHESTER (1985, 2020, 2022, 2023, 2024)

Hulme estate walkways and rat runs/High/Ordinary shops with security wire at the counter – any purchase is passed through small grille – no chance running off with that can of beans. It's all a can of worms huh/ Burnt out cars – inspiration for torch songs, perhaps/ Atmospheric decay/Hulme Labour Club, my band play with some Factory Records group – packed and fun/ Fred Vermorel, an old friend of Malcolm McLaren's, tells me that he misses Tony Wilson more than he does Malcolm. I can imagine/I read and talk twice at the Louder than Words *literary festival – aptly, near to Tony Wilson Place. RIP.*

Soundtrack: A broken record. Needle trapped in endless groove. Somehow arriving at fresh beat and flow of its own.

Disassembling location, manifold angles of approach. Total art.

Psyche pushed into interior – the gift of narcissism and conceit that keeps giving. And taking.

Drugged existence is eerie fantasy of otherness. Cheap tearjerker.

Stink of old displacement. Seeping from every crack in street/wall.

Fiction romance – a personal myth, therefore absolute and true. Verifiable.

Dogs fucking in the street – stuck together afterwards like the crowd trapped in its own desperate sway.

Sex: Ancoats. Display of naked gauche seriousness which makes more flippant people uncomfortable.

People wonder if there a self-hating undercurrent in post-modern culture. Or, a gesture of sorts?

Barrier blocks of empty apartments, cleared out riverside warehouses, motorways at full velocity, haunted power stations and chemical factories – underground places, uninhabitable spaces.

City grins to show its gums; ashen and marked by the angry border of red where teeth lean into each other, displaying deep roots. Grin widens.

T-shirt slogan on the street: Society is a plastic flower.

Dialogue: Is this a porn script?

Hunched up in a leather jacket. When hard work is play.

Cynical self-obliterating hostility. A cruel touch.

Timeless image: Plastic black and white aesthetic.

Dialogue: After sex can I eat a little?

City is partly seen, partly slept through – a new wave 60s futuristic movie. But not the movie I seem to say it is.

The city is continuous poem that is told by and to itself, as habit.

Dialogue: Next year I'll switch off and burn my bridges.

Dialogue: I'll wake up and forget that there had ever been any other option.

People want narrative disruption, mixed genres, interpolation of non-artist texts and documents, and perspectival shifts.

A flat, ironic tone works well in most city situations.

T-shirt slogan on the street: Once there was a god. A vicious god.

Top ten benefits of living in the city ranked:-

1. Déjà fait psychic repossession.

2. Residue of dream blurring.

3. Leitmotif of returning from the grave.

4. Form of hypnotic research.

5. Fear and utter tension.

6. Brazen bright colours created externally for internal mood shift control.

7. Moreish artificial cravings.

8. Mass psychic projection.

9. Subliminal images of low level acceleration and jarring trauma.

10. Daily/hourly derailment.

Dialogue: Maybe you'll choose the man on the bed in the next room...

Man in pub thinks the reply to any question worth knowing the answer to takes too long to tell. Closed, cold lips.

Passer-by unable to observe the breakage of

everything; the wear and the tears.

Atmosphere: Movement captured by surveillance camera. Heading right at the wall, going at 100 miles an hour.

Soundtrack – Chopin's *Prelude in E Minor* (the second saddest of all keys, perhaps).

City is a three-act structure with insistence on closed ending. Dead end.

Sex: She says, I couldn't love anyone if my life depended on it – sad truth: It doesn't.

There are two types of people – those who want to laugh ironically, and those who are already laughing ironically.

People are into the film *The Wilds Angels* because it includes the truism: *to keep on living is just to keep on paying the rent.*

T-shirt slogan on the street: Dread and ghosts.

Most people are in a terminal yet indefinite state of being at a loose end.

People in street (Hulme) laugh at idea of neurotic misery. The only way to be.

Tension tension tension pause tension tension tension pause. Repeat. Perfect articulation of the energy.

People are waiting. Waiting is a conjuring trick accomplished by magicians every day.

The interaction between social space, perception and exposure is flecked with low level, occasionally hysterical violence.

Dialogue: I love the feeling of getting someone to make me come, without making them come in return. A pure feeling.

Dialogue: Self-loathing... is that me?

Out in the rain, out on the very edge. There are certain things that cannot be reached.

Of remembrance: Reading the sharper signs, leaning into the vague signals.

People look at their own sadness and find it to be real.

Dialogue: I would quite like to believe in it all again.

Where does the City end? Where does it begin. Do you believe in the city?

People believe that the city is a movie about what the modern world really means.

The city lives in photographer's aesthetic, forming sense of grand guignol. The image develops its own life.

The city will only accept those who no longer daydream about it.

Total surveillance culture always welcomed by narcissists. A reason to comb your hair. Neat.

The sound of the city is of an endless drone. This detracts from the purity of the image, people say.

People are in love with the secret sublime allure of the city. *You don't understand.*

They say (dialogue): My dealer is at that party.

People cock their fingers like a gun. And look in the mirror. Firing blanks.

Passer-by looking for a clues where to go says faces are as suggestive as signs. Faces *are* signs.

People say: Watch us fade to black.

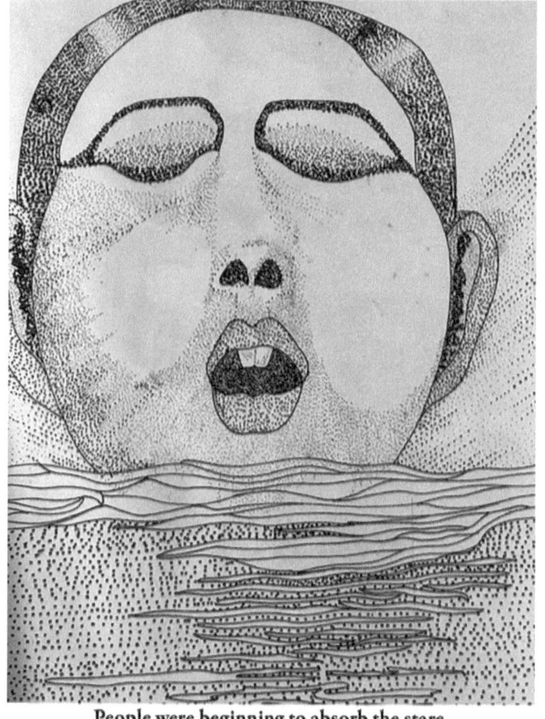

People were beginning to absorb the stare.

MARSEILLES (2019)

Brutalism. We stay in Corbusier's 1952 block La Cité Radieuse, his first Unité d'Habitation – 'Arguably the most influential Brutalist building of all time.' A city inside a block of flats, *the idea of which, according to Corbusier's statement, is to create: 'A machine for living in.' He also said: 'Made for men, it is made to the human scale. It has also the robustness which is inherent in modern technique, and it shows the new splendour of bare concrete.' I love concrete – bare. Stunning. I'm still feeling it.*

Atmosphere: Swirls and coils, conspicuous and painstakingly rhythmic. Rhythm is always the key.

Sex: Afterwards, dreams become as impenetrable as death. Death as koan. Dream as koan.

Café: Woman sips coffee. Thinks she can put ideas into the world. Vernacular insinuates something behind itself.

City floats on clouds of metafiction. Comfortably. No joins. *Inauguration of the Pleasure Dome.*

People filmed in projects in jagged tone of noir and bathos – reels shown in contemporary arrangement. Nice.

Surface simplicity. Emotional undercurrents consoling and alienating simultaneously. Display of spiritual ambition.

People drink all day in the red sun. Black moon is lopsided. Some tears flow.

Silver pathos of life makes mouths dry. Glamour is fear – golden.

Downwards glances on street. People look for disembodied ghosts of chances. Pavement as funhouse mirror.

Sunrise so beautiful that nothing can hurt anyone. Lovers suffer any and all abasement.

City is an only child forever trapped in own reverie. Solitary. But forever centred.

City is shards and shapes pieced together in bad urban geography. Beautiful.

 People strive to prove utter devotion to the objects of their adoration.

People have sex like American B movies.

City: Emptied out frame. Composition portrays both buildings and landscape with equal standing. Surpassing mysteries.

Tensions render the streets catatonic. Followed after a period with slow motion words, assembled with suspense.

Dialogue: By living in the city you will become familiar with the nature of chance. 'Toute révolution est un coup de dés.'

Like Jim Morrison, the city trembles over any activity that appears to have no meaning.

Gazing out at sea. A gift of the sense of infinity that is an end itself. Documentary scenes faked for sake of romance.

Guy beats up wife. He could've killed her right there. Woman does not know how to scream.

Street as theatre. City is actor. Role play. Onlookers are audience. Audience want agony. Actor becomes masochist.

The guy beating up his wife. He says, you can't ask an actor to make a moral judgement about the character he's playing. His wife now screams.

Metaphysical suicide, says Sartre, smoking.

Twenty thousand cut up words drifting like dub.

Passers-by go round and round in the sun, devoured by flames. Looking for everything lost or left behind.

Eighty three per cent of people live in a constant state of hot melodrama of boredom.

The performance or ritual of appropriate rites for souls in limbo.

People laugh at the fate of their friends. Freudian concept of destiny as replacement for parental agency. Visible like distant glow in lurid Oedipal hues.

Sometimes, the city allows in only those who have forfeited, squandered, or mislaid desire.

The street: Where something may or may not have happened. Woman puts on sunglasses and tries to smile.

Man says to other man (dialogue): So it's *you*.

City is not troubled by the idea of reasoned evaluation. City is not concerned with chronology.

Dialogue: The real sadness of people's misfortune is that there's *nothing* to be done.

Man removes clothes. First floor apartment. Woman, naked also, looks. Thinks: his skin is the colour of cigarette smoke. Mirror is blurred.

Morning. Drawn curtain. Noise of rubbish trucks. Muscles move in tender back. Pulsing in time with heartbeat. Nobody is coming.

City sleeps in funeral pose. Flower arrangements in park as wreaths. Nobody is coming.

T-shirt slogan on the street: Is death necessary?

T-shirt slogan on the street: Cowardice and violence forever.

Naked mannequins in shop window. Context: Spirits, gods, planes.

Introducing existentialism. Late Night Show take.

People would like to make more art movies.

NEW YORK (1989, 2023, 2024)

I live for a while with Warhol/Factory photographer Nat Finkelstein (Nat the Hat, as he was known by the Silver Factory people), vaguely round the corner from Bleeker Street, home of famous Bleeker Bob's record shop – where I/we never shop (I fictionalise this period in my novel Looking for a Kiss*) /Hanging out at various clubs – Red Zone, Save the Robots etc, at some bars – the Scrap, for instance, and at the Chelsea Hotel, with Club Kids and artists/Later, we launch two of my books* Disorderly Magic and Other Disturbances *(Far West Press) and the aforementioned* Looking for a Kiss *(PC-Press) in the city – in Bushwick and the East Village, respectively.*

City picks up speed and scale throughout, and flares – cells intertwining freely in and out of one another like the being they constitute.

Passer-by says: American nightmare is unforgiving. Stating the obvious is greatest transgression in poetry, film, city.

Black magician A Crowley esq. curses *call no man happy till he's dead or at least has left New York.* Black magician is himself cursed.

People say there are two sorts of people in the city. And they only meet when they are dead or in bed. Figuratively speaking.

Woman in midtown restaurant says calculator needed to count fictions and deceptions she has told herself.

Popularity seekers. Masturbatory contemplation of a remote object of fantastic desire.

Large department store windows act as mirrors that become instruments of regret for passers-by who cannot resist looking. Cruel demonstration of psychological dynamics.

Woman adds: Art provides sustenance and solace, but not for long. ... easy come...

City says real life is just performance art. Like *Arthur Rimbaud in New York*.

People in clubs go home to flush away the drugs in their coats. But suddenly remember there are *No More Coats and No More Home*.

Everywhere: People turn their hats into crowns.

Sound of city: Muffled like listening through double glazing. Time clock of the heart paused. Reaction not contained by limits.

Everyone wants to live in places with 70-foot vaulted ceilings, tombstone floors, exposed brick, underneath spiritual flights paths. Large TV set.

Composition: Cadence and angles. Woman in bar remembers a dream story. The glass moves on its own.

Dialogue: As to the old way of life what will you do with it?

No umbrellas needed in this singing rain.

Dialogue: I've got nothing I need right here.

Woman in restaurant says she thinks we are near to the wellspring that brought the world into being.

Everyone walks like they are uptight in black plastic sunglasses

Man in bar says history isn't polemical it's essentially

glorification. Other man says history is really an avalanche.

People in the streets are interested in fragmentation – arranging those fragments nearer to where they live.

Passer-by thinks other people are collapsing stars. Wishful thinking.

Passer-by thinks gold at end of rainbow is actually silver. Andy Warhol told him.

Astro America. Menacing charm while searching for the dynamic.

Indifferent sequence of signs – rites on the street.

T-shirt slogan on the street: Utopia achieved.

Backwash elaborations – high temperature fissions and visions.

Man says he knows the immensity and radiance of it all.

Man in bar buys drink – the price: cynicism and knowledge beyond words.

Street. Territory sampled and scrambled back in bits and pieces.

City of unspooling film: Narrative device – dramatis personae put in difficult predicament/Escape/But only to even more punishing predicaments/Again and again/The end.

Man says (Dialogue): Fuck the cosmic overview.

City as restaurant. Speciality: The slow grilling of the lost over open flame. Cooking time: Forever.

Rumour: People feel that all authentic connections are discontinued, outdated.

A lowdown story. Exotic alarm on.

Dialogue: I am an artist. I sell my love.

People are unsure about which jacket to wear to create a tone. Some wear Danny Fields' jacket.

Outlines upon pale shadows and still more pale, becoming pixilated.

Art in boxes. Corpses in boxes. Discrete arrangement.

Punchline: I might even show up myself someday.

Dialogue: I'm $100 dollars from complete breakdown. How about you?

People live in dead houses. Chimneys blow baffling smoke signals, like Lee Scratch Perry. Pfft.

Negative Girl says city is accidental. Does not create anything. Just collections of notes and noises. City is the music can you play when you can't play.

T-shirt slogan on street: Hanging w/ Bill and Jean-Michel and Victor B.

Dialogue: I can feel the vibrations of lucky people.

City/movie. Dramatis personae merely markers in the presentation of idea.

Image drifts in sky over city. Visible even from subway underworld.

Delirium and magnetic emanations. Between the

shadows of leaves in the wind

Dialogue (social media): *New York is such an ugly place. I hear everyone in my head, constantly, even alone in a room... impossible to shut it out. Impossible.*

Sometimes city talks in words. Other times not at all.

There is defiance in stillness, city thinks.

Woman in café says she is an invisible observer. I like her.

The only things of interest that ever happen occur in rented, temporary spaces. New interior desires.

Sarcasm of man in bar prompts everyone else to leave. Barman bar locks up. Gives man the keys.

Camera pulls back, shows cityscape. Horizon is final. But not the end.

T-shirt slogan on the street: The city is elsewhere.

Dialogue: These are the facts about what happened to me from the moment I ran away from home...

City is a poem. Charles Bukowski says he isn't sure whether *it's good poetry or bad acid.*

T-shirt slogan on the street: I'm a hypocrite not a liar.

T-shirt slogan on the street: Now they can hide an H-bomb in the sky.

Artists in lofts say: We are all Mary Magdalene, giving it all away.

Downtown art crowd reflect only on structure of consciousness and extreme pornography.

Passers-by have all the urgency of rethinking today.

Dialogue: I was howling and began fucking whoring...
fucking and whoring.

Hoaxes in boxes piled up in living rooms, balconies,
altars and antique stores.

Man says city isn't a place or a movie or a painting,
it's a play about the rehearsal of a play. Like in that
film we saw once. But it's hard to engage without an
audience.

City stages its own disaster.

Woman wears ring on her finger of melted silver,
gold and dreams – it's a dying city, she says – just like
Kathy Acker.

Tracking shot shows all the usual directions are
irrelevant.

PALERMO (2023)

My favourite structures are the ramshackle shops and stalls selling cheap fruit and food –the buzz is free – on the filthy market streets with which the city is blessed/ Also, there's the Massimo Theatre, built in 1897, the biggest theatre in Italy and the third biggest in Europe – engraved on the architrave is the phrase: 'Art renews people and reveals their life. Love of art is useless where it does not seek to prepare for the future.'

Rotten fruit bursting forth like the god damned sun.

Wry, decompressed altitude and abstraction – uncommon sense taken to the point of revelation. Alien even to itself.

A sun up to sun down refusal to guard the truth. Shifting centre where no one's imagination would ever leave them alone.

Dialogue: We will be turned into monuments.

Street: An avalanche of real things. Energy probes to find way in, and out again.

City works like delicious and potent drug – solidity melts away. Extent of flow taken into all accounts.

Artist says: Intellect lacks transcendent facet. Artist screws and paints – says: Look and learn. Aura gets ahead of artist.

Woman in bar says city is art. Says city is in agony because of beauty. Says beauty cannot come from happiness. Says: Only from its opposite. City in act of creation is always in misery.

Sex: Tension. In the throat like a gasp, or a moment of inspiration.

People desire both embrace and unease. People already in the deep end.

The bigger picture is cartoon, or hasty child's sketch. In the background: drugged skies. Aesthetics of the irrational.

Sex: Sweat licked from naked back for the drug rush. Detour of instinct.

Someone uttered and nearly listened and nearly responded. People have no weight at all. Among envious ruins.

Homeless man in vast cold space reaches dirty hand out for first clean shard of sunlight at daybreak.

Dialogue: My price is other peoples' values.

T-shirt slogan on the street: I don't want to win anything.

People pray to some gods above and below for different experience of the passage of time sometime.

Man says thieves want to sell his stolen life back to him – cheap at half the price.

Dialogue: Let me show you something else.

People search for value: Certain beauty in the streets.

Hedonist escapes those things that have been ascribed to her. Nothing is fixed. Attachment of individuality to artifice.

People think life in city is an eternal below job.

Man says descendants of Baudelaire are right: City is

strung out on fibre optic nerves.

Mean city is compressed beyond flux and sensation. Those glances all day.

Elsewhere: Carnival sex and papier maché skeletons. There's nowhere left to go.

Artists search for raw materials with guaranteed results. They fuck like robots.

Woman says (Dialogue): A particular world is passing away right in front of my eyes. It is better than most, but not all, TV.

Whisper passes through thin air. Air becomes thinner.

Bar: World travellers' tales of misplacement and knowing. High protein.

Things are burning. Ash darkens sky. Mottled sun reflects the main tendencies of the time.

Woman seeks next uncertain place. Receives message from Jacques Derrida.

You sob.

T-shirt slogan on the street: The stakes are never yourself.

The stakes are always yourself.

Street is holy: The blessings of loud, insistent words.

Dialogue: He treats me like a rag doll.

T-shirt slogan on the street: Things are against us.

Bored woman in café writes: When everyone wants

to be known: Vanish.

Sex: Art school connections make her come.

Passers-by feel that there is little or no reason to think that they might be falling apart just like everyone else.

Common or garden artist becomes Cubist – primal issues, primal point.

Woman looking over her balcony, tells herself sad stories. The ending is a jump cut.

Stinking rubbish piled high in the streets and alleyways. Under the skin.

Woman thinks deeply about theory of Resistentialism which asserts: *things are against us*. This feeling is confirmed by the Clark Trimble experiments involving toast and marmalade dropped onto various carpets. Tests demonstrate that the more expensive the carpet, the higher the incidence of marmalade landing downward. City is Resistentialist, woman thinks, limping.

Crowded beach. Supernatural emanations.

Sign somewhere points to: Dark psychological underground.

Conditions for an efficient spontaneity. A form of time travel.

A strategy of and for pessimism – *everyone* can predict the future.

People want: Spiritual protection, manmade phantoms, a slip in time, biofeedback, transcendental irritation.

People now interested only in *ecstatic* form of disappearance.

The behaviour of everybody and everything.

PARIS, ST ETIENNE, LILLE, BORDEAUX (1972, 2006, 2011, 2021 etc – several visits over the 80s, 90s, etc)

Wine/ In St Etienne I stay with family, one of whom suffers from alcoholism, which sometimes expresses itself in bouts of pulling out his own hair – with his wild tufts sticking up, I think of him as the archetypal deranged poet set to self-destruct/Paris – I write the poem 'Music I Listened to in My Head While Walking Around the Jean-Michel Basquiat Exhibition at the Le Musée d'art Moderne de la Ville de Paris on 22/01/11', featured in the book Disorderly Magic and Other Disturbances *(the one-line foreword to which is written by eminent Parisian artist Sylvie Selig – La Biennale de Lyon, etc. I visit her in the Montmartre apartment which she shares with her wild creations – 'the weird family').*

People feel let down. They say that modern artists should convey the same universal meaning. No meaning at all.

People say that beauty has an evaporated essence – like poetry.

Artists may fail – but not to recall. Concealed context.

Dialogue: The brain and body are the puppet and the ego is the puppet master. There is no twist?

Good taste is death, vulgarity is life. People have taken Mary Quant's sentiment to heart.

Sex: Vulgarity is life. Good taste is death.

Rumour: On this street, Daniel Cohn-Bendit – Danny the Red – said: *I am myself. The hot centre of things.*

Criminality as artistic brand. Ongoing experiment in

authenticity. High speed collision on the street.

T-shirt slogan on the street: Forget art and success.

People believe that insanity and sadness are tools. They are aware that the Loa enters believers.

T-shirt slogan on the street: Respect and fear my mambo.

Little or no poetry to be distilled from certain experiences. Everything plainly visible in lurid Electral colours

People live on barren soil. Language like minimalist architecture. Concrete freedom.

Man and woman walk down street minding the psychic gap like a neurotic Bergman couple.

Street. Transition is relief, arrival: Flat. Limits exceeded.

People worry about betraying reality. *Vive le resistance*.

Dialogue (Montmartre): We live in a city on the kill.

Artists refuse to drink out of any modish glassware that has not been designed by Antonin Artaud.

People prefer surprise effects over meaning to fit narrative.

The Projects: Acrophobia. Cause and effect. Psyche opposes the world.

Atmosphere. Multi flow of AC/DC power. Sparks in lieu of meagre images and forms of other things. Unreal montages.

Dialogue: ... And which has the most appealing aroma?

Direction: The uncharted occult inhabited by figurative spirits.

The street drifts. Heroic beatitudes and agonised expressions.

Dialogue: If I'm not touched it is impossible to live.

People exist in nameless areas and stretch themselves out in front of other people's lives.

There is an acceptance only of those artists who acknowledge life with a defining sensibility.

Questions: Can everything be poetically conceived? How valuable is fragility?

Favourite substitute for life. Plastic? Rubber? Leather?

But you are unremembered. Recollections buried in rubble of ruined hacienda – which, yes of course, must be rebuilt.

The poetry of the hermeneutic code, proairetic code, cultural code, connotative code, and symbolic code lasted fifty years. Or more.

The street pushes imagination into motion. The past falls, stretches and shines. Like plastic rubber leather.

The street flaunts its scars. Mythology as form of vertigo.

Woman in café cuts up magazines for collages with eyes closed. Divine blueprints for un/imaginative future.

Rhythm as instinctive gesture. Psyche as real as the city.

Dialogue (gothic): I am a dead and shrouded figure, stone-like and still, conveying the finality, the point at which the shroud covers all, and the material world falls away.

Passer-by rejects rationalist worldview. Divided dark and light. Seduced by moonlit chaos.

Dialogue: You don't know what I'm going to do today and neither do I.

Streets negotiated by poet skeletons. The city belongs to those who can dream it, as they say.

T-shirt slogan on the street: Constant desire dead.

Woman in café – red wine – says she is interested in the sacred and profane.

T-shirt slogan on the street: Beautiful nightmare right here.

Some people think that the only car to drive in city is a white Ford Galaxy.

Night people scavengers. Criminal ascendancy. Low crowd, not unglamorous.

People wonder if artists are fractured by post modernism, dispersed in firmament.

Man walks on tightrope – thin line between splendour and gravity. Falls.

Man walks with his eyes to the ground. Mapping the loneliness and expression of private sorrows.

City: Set in full moonlight, before the Flood.

Pop statement.
Slender line slacks, jeans, beachwear, shirts, swimwear.

ROME, NAPLES, LECCE, ANZIO, THE AMALFI COAST (1990, 2021, etc)

In Rome I am blessed by Pope Benedict XVI (born Joseph Aloisius Ratzinger)/And hang out a little in Trastevere with Sex Pistols tour manager John Tiberi, who lives in Rome part time/In Puglia I borrow and crash a policeman's BMW. I watch him unconsciously stroke his holstered pistol as he surveys the damage.

City in sunlight shines like phosphorous.

Phosphorescent fires against a sepia framed backdrop.

Break it up. Aesthetics in freefall signal decline.

T-shirt slogan on the street: A skeleton in whose closet?

City floats on Zen-like appreciation and spiritual acceptance, Or, avoidance of articulating a particular point.

Fabulous origins of myths projected into silver sky by the foaming tail of comet. Lengthened into the past.

Objects that speak (no need for dialogue): trap door, rubber floor, black and white stills from Italian cinema.

People live at the broken edge of the map. Man walks out of the door.

The movie's impact arrives through the tight scrutiny of behaviour. Audience aware of events and narrative w/out need for definition.

Like Patti Smith the city seeks *the nerves under your skin*.

Passer-by worries about place in the bigger picture. His jacket is unbuttoned. His kisses are cigarette breaths. Sweet.

City wants people to pull apart screen separating life and art. City wants honest entertainment. Value for money.

Like poets who got to despise literary expression, who have the insight but loathe its pronouncement.

T-shirt slogan on the street: How do I work out how dispose of the future?

Movie takes place in endless teeming rain. Arid stone and concrete is marked and blemished. Men in café look through streaked window.

Sex: Her profound desires. *So it's you.* Whistling in the wind.

Woman invents a language in order to understand some peculiar energy from the streets in hidden and brilliant corners.

Man semi-mesmerised but cool. With nonchalant link to state-of-art circuitry. Last fading remnant of modernity. Killed every night.

Acknowledging that it is no longer possible to say anything keeps the lonely company.

T-shirt slogan on the street: I now want everything that happens to me to happen now.

Dialogue: Recently, I have been picturing other visions of charm and magnetism.

The film is about the pits we entomb ourselves in. The viewer has psychological suture.

A large mirror which filters and rearranges every image. Principal events now easier on the eye.

Woman in café. Screwed up piece of paper on floor. She leaves. I unscrew her paper and read: The carnage is sublime.

The sequence is unforgettable: Stage, screen and scene.

Woman on metro looking for: *Brand new revenge.*

Dialogue: *Tell your sister I'll throw bricks with her.*

The cult of the dead is goal orientated.

Dialogue: That would be obscene.

Italian miracle: The light in the window has terrifying lustre.

City demands elevation every single day.

Life on a promise: Spiritual city will reveal itself to you when you find yourself in that moment.

Man halted in his tracks, says: *Ah, that is me after all.*

Strange silent phone calls. Apocalyptic ring tone.

People in bars talk about concept of the open film. Woman looks for a place to sit down.

Man looks at his face in mirror of a parked car. Despises neo-realism. Everyone looks the same.

People leave the city and look in rear view mirror for sense of possibility.

Dialogue: I am no longer in love and I believe I never was.

City wears a halo/crown of thorns. Shadows in Plato's cave.

People lie down low in art house cinemas. Dust. Storiless.

People think better and have better sex in completely empty rooms readied for arrival or departure.

City in its loneliness transforms memory into lie.

City is whispers. Turning speech into puzzle. Unreliable narrator.

People vote yes for fresh era of customised interior design.

People and their frozen flesh melt.

TIJUANA and ENSENADA (1987)

My original 1987 diary entry: 'Tijuana – a shock – a shanty town – like a rickety film set that was built for a shoddy/Shady film noir that real people then moved into. No real roads, rather large tracks that we bump along. No real signs – we unexpectedly find ourselves going the wrong direction down a one-way street with a mass of angry traffic heading our way. An allegory almost. A town infamous for its Donkey Shows – purported events where a woman engages in sexual acts with a donkey but are probably set ups to fool the US tourists stupid enough to drink in the various bars lining the main street – the corny Bar New York, Bar Hollywood, etc. We find it hard to get out of this town for some reason, going round in circles...' [Further excerpts from my original LA diary are included as an appendix.]

Atmosphere: Myth of morbid enervation.

Passer-by radiates heat and tension. Tendon in neck vibrates.

Camera on the perimeters – focus repositioned away from the living edge. Now hovering.

Everything without name. Traversing half understood images. Like hieroglyphic symbols.

Disorderly logic of a bad dream. Everything is askew and unavoidable.

The view: Amyl nitrate sunrise. And sky with two moons.

Bad luck in the air – and it is being breathed in by you.

Woman over there, watching, is silver shard of the small and the astray and is the entire city. There is zero upshot moral.

People bound to the particular fetters of the city.

Mood: Terror tactics and secret manoeuvres.

Street: Sadomasochist interaction – the more it hurts the more real it is for you.

A rattlesnake, a rotation of sun beams its lengths, stark alleys, sunset – moonlight on effigies in public spaces – pictures of signs.

Close up: A mouth. Chapped lips. Open. Brown teeth. Some missing. Furred tongue. Camera moves back. Fingers soiled, thickened, tough, tear off chunks of broca, stuff pastry into mouth. Distended. Open.

Tower of babel voiceover, hard corps hi-tech New Worldism, codewords to the underground. Requiem for a dream.

T-shirt slogan on the street: I can nullify any dream.

City: Heat exhaustion could never be taken for a thoughtful demeanour. I put on my sunglasses.

People laugh – but not simultaneously.

Dialogue: I'm more than enough.

Bar: Straight ahead sentimental stories. Smile.

People reconstruct mysterious actions. Aware of need to stay vigilant of the span of time.

Looking at map is to imagine another lost world.

Melancholia.

Concealed space is holy only because of the completeness it processes. Nothing else matters.

People in the solitude claim direct line to all the sorrow in the world. As the crow flies.

People put creative faith in magical realism. Triggers of association to whatever game is being played.

T-shirt slogan on the street: As ugly as chance.

Dial on Chrysler stereo is moved slowly from left to right, from right to left. Mariachi and bones.

Dialogue: ... around our shoulders embracing will to sleep tight and perish in the car without waking up. Sand will drift into the room the whole city will be covered under the sand falling from the sky until the tallest buildings have drowned.

People have awareness of inconsequential absurdity. Beyond city limits.

Man makes light of how infinite journey cleanses. Distance, again.

All to be found, all to be discounted. Admittedly there is the primal shock.

City centre. Put hands up for point of no return.

Then there are the faces.

Passer-by looks on ground, but not up at sky, for clue beyond the material world.

Sex: I saw white. Did you? A lie/A line: Yes.

Street: People step on the violent shadows.

City: Is so sad that the rain has changed colour and the dogs no longer lay down.

Street: Flows in to the gutter, at the end of which is another gutter.

T-shirt slogan on the street: There is no beautiful friend anywhere.

No one is really too concerned with material representations of divinity.

City: Like the world and everything, assembled carelessly.

Rumour: There is no road anywhere.

City: Some places exist only because people have sung about them.

Dialogue: There is nothing wrong with me.

Atmosphere: Silence as loss of balance.

Soundtrack: Dub plate version of US psychedelia plus 50s minimalism.

People step out of their skins. To become the other.

T-shirt slogan on the street: I am you. You are dead.

Dialogue: I'm having a really heavy trip right now, you know?

Spectral moon is a remote spirit. Cheap tearjerker.

Skill: Knowledge of exactly how much malevolence needed to just keep going.

City life is a sequence of low value transactions. Genuine despair.

Dialogue: Who can be patient enough to wait until life returns?

City alters assumption of what cities should be like.

Some people somewhere born and live in the debris. Tra-la-la.

It all starts with flickering lights, portentous music, electric utterance explaining something about reality. SFX kitsch. Hi-tech screen terror.

The finale is: ride into sunset, burning motorcycle on the roadside, locking eyes for the last time, the intruder entered house, standing in front of a setting sun, the referee gets to a 10 count, the freeze-frame of a haunted face, car is pulled out of the swamp, frozen in terror as credits roll, a fast close-up on both characters just before the shooting starts, touching reunion between the two on a beach, a complete bloodbath with few survivors, and the question: Who is financing this film anyway?

People break out of film's location and hit the open road. No end in sight. Somewhere.

Language symbol image.

Pop statement. Do you have any ideas?

WARSAW and KRAKOW (1967, 2077, 2022, etc)

I was born in the UK but come from a Polish background. My father was born and lived in Jazlowiecka, eastern Poland, and my mother in Sutkowszczyzna, eastern Poland, small villages near Lwow/Lviv, now part of the Ukraine. I myself recently received Polish citizenship. My parents, along with their families, were ethnically cleansed from their homes in 1940 by the Soviets, and transported to Siberia – 19 months of hard labour, starvation, and disease, at the Monastyriok work camp in the Kotlas area of Archangelsk. After the war, they settled, via Uzbekistan, Persia, Palestine, Uganda, in the UK – a real journey.

Then it began to rain.

Futile revolt of a world which leans to the cogent arrangement of all ingredients of life.

Haunting score: Everything is as I desire it to be – as long as I don't desire it to be something different.

People think they want to jump out of a high tower (The Palace of Culture and Science – Pałac Kultury i Nauki) and watch silver steel sputniks spunking up the skies.

Milk bar: Woman has had a permanent spell cast over her.

Priest gives absolution for all sins except hope.

City question: Where is the gestalt created?

Spatial psychology: Repetition that life is marvellous.

Street: Spectacular performances by secret actors. Anonymity of the type.

Everything so uptight that something has splintered.

People look like blurred extras in European art house film. Not merely an underlying comment about society.

The city knows that the catastrophe and rupture is beautiful.

Stylistic nihilism is a drama of bewilderment.

Interaction with the city is so blurred that it doesn't matter where people are.

Dialogue: You have to keep moving fast so people don't point at you.

A bell rings endlessly. Absolute emergencies surprise even the future. Echo moving in sync.

Dialogue: I write history in the first person. Not the third.

The possibility of nostalgia does not entirely convince.

Angel of death beats its black wings. Angel hates parks and slippery morgue floors.

Passers-by say audience is not important, the audience is after the fact.

The city is a continuous poem that never rhymes.

Dialogue: I found everything is in touch with beauty and if there was disorganisation then it was an organisation of the disorganisation, which is just another form of organisation.

City is a dance: 'Couple face one another holding inside hands (man R girl L), free hand extended,

slightly below shoulder level, palm inwards, fingers curved.
Beginning outside feet (man L girl R) take one step.
Hop on outside foot swinging inside leg from hip across outside leg; swing back in opposite direction hopping again on outside foot.
Repeat above in opposite direction changing hands and commencing on outside feet (man R girl L).
Repeat bars one to 4.
Ballroom hold; eight poker steps clockwise polka.
The dance may be repeated as often as desired.'

T-shirt slogan on the street: I am the truth not the facts.

People strive to attain the religious and holy state of detached indifference.

The film is a bad tragedy and the only one who doesn't know is the hero. Without him there is no movie.

Street: Ash and embers. Man meets woman. Heart bursting in vacuum.

Woman demands that the fantastic at borders of imagination is opened. Unconscious desires fulfilled.

Sadist – her cheerfulness hurt.

City: Spiritual possibilities of the horror film.

Central nervous system affected by sequence of disturbances. But loss of emotional control successfully avoided.

Punchline: In other words it was a story with no narrative. The best kind.

Happy ever after household tableau as pantomime and dramatic performance following rules of stagecraft for full effect.

Man tells woman he wants to be ruined forever. She is suspicious. Strange digressions taken.

In time, endless greatness has the same effect as endless tedium.

Soundtrack: The sounds of an exorcism.

Woman casts spell that will stop city in its tracks.

Mood: Praying to ancient saints for a new life in an intimate space.

Dialogue: The truth is that waiting consists of many, many levels.

The city has elemental concerns. Spectacular rituals of ennui.

People in street wade through wake raised by the tide of crushed hopes. Spectacular rituals of ennui.

City people dream another, different city closer to their hearts.

Life in city is repetition of same dispersion every day. Black and white (dis)passion play.

Like sight of own asshole, people always wonder what their heads look like from above. People astrally project.

People survive in the city by expertly wielding their helplessness.

Rich people spend all their money on release from the past. Saturn returns.

People able to extend back along a current to alter past and remake themselves.

Here is found the classical idea that the amount of shed tears stored in the deep well of the city always remains the same.

Woman in street tells a story – it refuses to/doesn't end.

Some people call for government censorship regarding the issue of inner states made exterior.

The only law in the city is 'the law of doom'. And law of diminishing returns.

People gather around each other because there is no one else. Those people could, and often are, ourselves.

The film of/as the city always ends. Ending is a brazier of charms in the city rubble (of memory)

Then it begins to rain.

'Have image will travel'.

APPENDIX 1

This piece was originally written for and published in the anthology Pretty Obscure *(Far West Press, 2024). It's the stylistic prototype for the pieces in this book.*

CREATIVE DIRECTORY/TAXONOMY (EXCERPTS) – NEW YORK (EAST VILLAGE/ WEST VILLAGE/BUSHWICK), (July 1989 and April 2023)

1. Unstable street is steadied by an utterance.
2. Poetic line advances. Impossible connections.
3. One image follows another – interfacing fluid mirror.
4. Uncapped bottle of beer – smudged lipstick.
5. Uncapped lipstick – smudged bottle of beer.
6. Sex. Holy prayer cards on bedside cabinet. Holy cards close to chest.
7. Poetics governed by impulse. *Yo Vito*!
8. Dialogue: I'm not scared! You're scared! I'm not scared.
9. Taxi ride at night. Link with words *en route*. [Timeless immobility].
10. Dialogue: You were going to tell me something before all this happened, what was it?
11. What does anyone want? To offer a raw-boned shoulder twisted against the world.
12. Phone booth. Man cries. Love is dead. Vibration travels from star to star.
13. Voodoo shops in Lower East Side. X marks the spot. Line between intuition, refusal, affirmation.

14. Extended dream sequence of bondage vignettes. Some words spoken: But I don't FEEL anything.
15. Everything is learnt from the night – weight and density of thoughts.
16. Your skin is so wonderful. Image of self. She said. Image of nylon.
17. New star visible via angel's eye.
18. Vertigo of modern sensibility. What lies beneath; the neural pit and electric crackle.
19. People believe in dread more than they believe in allure. They howl.
20. What do you want? Control of own mystery.
21. Life in the city is a balancing act: Hysterical crude illusionism. Dazed abstract psychology. Theory of misfortune.
22. Well, if you put it like THAT!
23. Question: Is the Parisian void *better* than the New York void?
24. Title moves between two different senses. Promise of explanation of some particular movement.
25. Image always bleeds faster than cash.
26. The glamor business: D and F ride through town. T asks M about the book she is starting. Magazine pages being turned over. Text against text.
27. This is not just an object, it's just an object. Archetype against archetype.
28. Violence of slow motion sentences. [Disappearance].
29. People live in a documentary style. Action is always quoted.
30. People have been working all day. Point of view: reverse shot only.
31. Dialogue: I will remember this moment for the rest of my life.
32. The street: Disney plus bodily fluids and open wounds.

33. What do you want? Control of your own misery.
34. Alone in a room. Turn light on and off. On and off. You can see the story.
35. Someone quotes: 'Frigid people really make it.'
36. Desire in eyes like dying words. Full face or in profile.
37. The street is: Cinematic paradox. Are you certain?
38. The history of the future. Hegel. (Hey girl). Nostalgia for the lost.
39. Dialogue: Wow! (of course)
40. The meeting of a client's need. Life with subtitles on.
41. Question: Do you know how to Pony?
42. Classical chiffon evening gowns. Woman's mouth open, eyes half closed. Uncertainty of interpretation.
43. Heat. Blurry and unfocused. Associations of the taste of old, used pornography.
44. Architecture is masked figure.
45. 'Purism' tattooed on thigh. Fiction is an under developed pretext.
46. Atmosphere: old 50s film. Movement between fragments/frames is called desire.
47. A new star visible. *Its Creator did not disdain.*
48. People quote Dante all the time: *Predestined turning point of God's intention.*
49. Wildest fantasies forever unfulfilled but always exceeded. Something else.
50. Movement towards something constantly absent. Travellers' tales.
51. People say Modernist film theory is the key to everything.
52. Freudian dream symbolism. Buildings dissolve as soon as approached.

53. Fixed aesthetic of street corner – inviting departures rather than arrivals.
54. Fact of flesh without flash. Pre-visual freedom.
55. Genuine religious feelings. Gears of consequence.
56. Disquieting lady makes escalating demands. Asks about philosophy of the bathroom.
57. Club Kids are full of prevailing climate of parochial formalism.
58. Dialogue: When I first met you I thought I might be dying. I thought it might be good.
59. Older man dreams of breaking into warehouses on Hudson River piers.
60. People simply love the anti-humanism of structuralism.
61. Steam engine unconscious. Loneliness. Neutral neglect.
62. Do you want art about art and signs upon signs?
63. Dialogue: They're collapsing, too... in perfect unison
64. Artists' lofts for rent. Artist imitates the viewer. Vacuum in an airless room
65. Everywhere. Walk on part – TV staging.
66. Dialogue: I can't look at you and breathe at the same time. (Extreme solitude).
67. People wonder if it's OK to have 'a sympathy for the abyss'.
68. Violence, how fluently it comes. How simply it cures you. Absence and the fast heartbeat.
69. People like eroticism through lack of context. Reflection and blankness find common identity.
70. Golden hour natural light and low sun sinking down on empty warehouses. Escape from worn out iconography.

71. Dialogue: Stop! Mama!
72. West Village. Woman in shop doorway reads battered copy of Tuli Kupferberg's *1001 Ways to Live Without Working*.
73. Club Kids in platform boots walking like monsters from Chelsea Hotel tell dealers to: fuck off. Snort face powder and blusher.
74. Sleeping in freshly wet bed. Moving beyond the embrace.
75. Arc of thin legs and bare arms. Distance from the feeling to the face.
76. Dialogue: Each and every attribute of society is my annihilation. (Folk joke).
77. Question. Images like jewels (momentum). Do you still believe in that?
78. Dialogue: Well say *something*.

LA DIARY – NOTES FROM BABYLON/THE FRONT LINE

Written in Los Angeles, spring 1987, at the age of 27, in a Silvine brand exercise book (which cost 19p, according to the price sticker which is still affixed to the cover) with a black felt tip pen (probably a Paper Mate).

... first sight from the plane: freeways crossing themselves... blood red sun setting. Down.

Airport huge, empty technology, looks like Luton carpark, near the bus station. No immediate heavy handed security. Hotels, eateries – many! – *Fatburger.*

A long drive, but you get used to it – an alien future city melting into freeway suburbs and then Hollywood – where the streets aren't paved with gold.

Apartment near Hollywood Boulevard – smooth, rich, part of a small block. Wooden polished floor, Alien Sex Fiend LP cover blown up into a picture on the wall, framed. Money. A Chagall print. Pretentions to culture, too. TV and video of course, tho' not extravagant. Everything in its proper place – no records strewn over the floor here. Astroturf on patio roof. Astroturf! Where are the electric sheep?

Hollywood Boulevard = Carnaby Street – full of tack. Grauman's – Bogart etc. Stars. Reagan's is outside a derelict shop. Lots of women with small feet.

They tore down paradise and.../Drive up to the hills/ Brutal rich houses/Huge bar/West Hollywood/Red berets – Angels patrol/Second-hand Levi's/Blue Thunder helicopter/Very powerful search light – into people's houses – in every dream home... someone's else's heartache [we found out later that a homeless man had been shot dead by the police as part of this incident]/Nearby apartments – one woman, G says, goes to bed *alone* every night, TV flickering in the darkness, sensearoundsurround tomb – loneliness/Laziness.

To the Scream club (Sacred Heart closed tonight)/Warehouse – big, like everything, 3 or 4 floors/No beer/Big bouncers, of course/Coke in the toilets, of course – a coke joke, yes/People slam to videos – Beastie Boys and, oh god, The Cult, a cross section of British cult bands – so boring/Boredom in the dark/None of this really suits LA – you don't say! – these images of death, heroin...

Drive to the Pacific/Coast road/Griffith Observatory/Venice – like Camden Market, baseball caps, Walkman's... lack/Street acts – rappers (bad), roller skaters/G says gang action but I felt no threat/Muscle beach people – extreme bodies fit for fuck all in extreme society/Nam vets – dirty, swathed in rotting war rags bumming fags and quarters – I gave a fag, but he deserved more.

John Lydon's house – X freaks! – five minutes from the beach, continental-style townhouse, windows open – X threatening to try and get in – 'Beware of the Kangaroo' sign in the window – wacky Lydon/Venice itself has a leafy village atmosphere – weird – criss-crossed by canals – plenty of laid back vibes – murals on the walls – rich but with a touch of cultural aspiration. Lydon's house is definitely an artist's house. The feeling: Everyone leave us alone, except the pizza man – fat white little Johnny waddling down to muscle beach – his type of irony, I suppose. [Weird that I wrote this – Lydon wasn't even fat at this time – clearly a premonition].

Way back/Freeway dreams/Stopped off at giant

Ralph's/'You have just made a verified saving'/'60 billion people served'/ Make that 60 billion and two – X and I stocked up on Ralph logo baseball caps, T-shirts, notebooks, etc [the PIL LP famously had taken the Ralph's graphic style and ran with it – and so did we].

PM – *Amadeus* on TV, pseudo-culture users attempted insight into Euro-genius hard-life-reality. Pfft.

Bus to the Pacific. Along Sunset, detour off through Westwood/UCLA – a quaint(ish) village scene going on/Off the strip into the suburbs – solid money, along curves.../ Pacific at sunset empty apart from few casual sunbathers – no one in the sea/Bus number 2 – 85c – met a guy from Eyrie Pennsylvania. He says: *life too fast fast fast in LA*, homeboy going back to Nowheresville even faster. We laugh – LA is the slowest place we've ever been to!/Bus to Venice, but had to change, got off at Santa Monica, a beach centre – the California girls are... the best/Jumped around in the sea – ocean! – I thought it would have been bluer. No pleasing some/Older lady says she moved here 40 years ago cause it was Paradise on Earth. Now Paradise Lost, says I. Not original I know.

Whole place feels like it has a giant glass dome over it – airless: like the air conditioned nightmare. Henry Miller where are you? And where are the artists? Culture is just TV/ But it's important to use that, I know.

We meet two Southend girls/Wide girls/Living off some guy near Highland – he pays their rent/They want into movies and on TV/ Ha!/The Lure – it still exists – *always*/They talked about doing a runner from hotels – always leave one empty suitcase in the room so they don't know you've gone.

On the beach writing/Think: no matter where you are/How much you travel/It's inside that matters – you have to sort your life out whatever/Wherever/Deep dreams huh – California-style/And what's life?/Writing on the beach? Or: *Achieve! Achieve! Achieve!* X is cracking up over the latter. So is G. So am I – but I don't want to just be part of the consumer nightmare – I want money – but I want to explode in fist fulls of *creative* $100 bills. Can I write for a living? What next?

Walk back to sunset – two and a half hours in the broiling red sun haze/Plastic and rubber on concrete and sand – we trudge/Surprisingly easy/Cool feet in stretch of beautiful Pacific/If you want to be specific, I'd die beside the Pacific – and never look back/Beachside dachas (smaller)/Hop skip and jump into the surf/The baby surfers have come to play, training for the jump to Malibu – yoo hoo!/Bus back to Formosa – cheeky driver: Behave! Mad Rasta guy says: What do you mean *behave*? The world's full of violence! Good night driver! Kaboom!/Yeah!

Laziness setting in/Getting up later/Now just sitting on AstroTurf roof garden – too hot to boogie/From here I can see: white Spanish hotel-style buildings, a high craggy shrub covered hill opposite, to the right... the sign... the great God: HOLLYWOOD.

Walk to second-hand bookshop – lots of cheap stuff – $2 – the usual books: Robert Anton Wilson's *The Earth Will Shake* hardback for $4 – I could spend all day here, all I'd need is money and a wheel barrow for the books/I imagine a small pocket of 'intellectuals' out here – a minority, like the punks or the transients, displaced persons – sneering and being sneered at by everyone else – or is it: cheerfully live and let live with no understanding? /Certainly gays seem to be getting more and more of a bashing – and racism in the colleges is hitting the news headlines – a KKK man in full costume walks through the campus – it's just a joke, he says. Everyone else just cares about their A grades.

TV/19 channels here/G just spends time flicking from one to another, not particularly watching anything – flashes of the Dodgers game, bits of *Green Acres*, cheesy sitcoms, programmes that show jewellery with a price tag that that you can phone in and buy, game shows with multi thousand dollar prizes, California Lottery – G says a fellow Mexican apparently won $14M, MTV (AOR/HM/BOWIE (day in day out)) – this is TV – life – too boring for sustained viewing, or people just can't keep their attention on anything for too long? Horrible.

Drive to Hollywood occult store/ What sort of current to be found there? Well, lots of expensive magical tack – nude figure candles, Anubis/antler skull skeleton, glass scrying balls – the meaningless ephemera of magic – for show – showbiz occult current flowing/Bought Thoth pack for $15.

PM - Kim Fowley's club/a few dollars to get in/No bar – this seems to drive people away, although those who are there look like they're enjoying it – what drug are they on? Fowley – a tall skin plus bones tired guy/Wired degenerate drug man with an unhappy look in his over-mascara'd eye flitting from front to back, space to space never seeming to find any rest or relaxation. A sick star on wane. Crowd – straight disco boppers, plus a bunch of trannies. Music: hi-energy disco, sub-Hippodrome rubbish. Spandau Ballet. You can imagine the excitement.

Griffith Observatory/Closed/Caves in the hills/ Dead end/There's a chink in the fence – shall we? We chicken out/What vagrant psycho hermit with his gang of Manson killers lives there? Or, what powerful Indian spirit hiding from the less powerful (?) gross god of false glamour resides there? – perhaps waiting to be set free by an earthquake – we don't want to know/Stop on hillside for view of Hollywood in its entirety – a stunning, shimmering, shaking sea of flickering yellow light pocked marked with white spots. A boom of visual Sensurround.

G is young enough to think that listening to *Raw Power* on a Cali beach means that he is one up on the other sun heads.

Boredom/X and I walk down Hollywood Boulevard – everything is stale and lacklustre – food shops – tacos, burgers, burritos – film books and poster shops that we can't be bothered to look at – a 1000 stars, or whatever, on the pavement and we walk over them regardless. Oblivious. Could not care less.

TV/MTV/Bowie day in day out/Dressed in his roller skates, leather new wave gear, singing a song with a social conscience. Yawn.

Venice/No sign of life in the Rotten home/Gang of rednecks shout: 'Your mummy didn't dress you right' at me. Fuck off/Buy a couple of pizza slices/ Lots of kids – beach/sun seems kind unbecoming to Yo Boy! attitude, same RE punk attitude I suppose, but they're not the sort to kick sand in anyone's face anyway. But ready for a ruck when drunk I'll bet. They own the beach. A crippled guy bad mouths X – and the kids all laugh. He does it to amuse them – he's their jester. His anger at the world spewing out in twisted grinning hate. Makes things interesting for the kids – he is a form of TV for the kids while they're away from their living rooms.

The ocean/Cold for first few seconds, then warm/ Foaming breakers/No one swims/Americans say it is too cold for them/They should try Hastings/Walk down to big rock jetty/I want to throw something in as an offering to the sea but a lifeguard shouts me away/I throw a stick in anyway, too hurriedly maybe – I wish for... *everything*.

Wearing a T-shirt now in wind and cold dusk/Only a dollar to our name and no shelter – no money plus ID required at bars anyway/Far away from home/Security in Formosa Ave/G and M not with us but on their way (maybe?!)/Isolation hits me/Slice of pizza fills out empty stomachs.

Hungover/Walk on my own down the Boulevard/Must train my powers of perception/Memory/Artistic-social awareness – which I don't have the remotest trace of today.

Melrose/walk down Sunset – everything and everyone spaced out/Looking for a side street into the Boulevard/Walk don't walk/Two guys ask for money/I ignore them and walk on – they look like they're thinking about their chances/Pretty good I'd say/I move on to the Boulevard/The gutter sleaze people are here – stars in their own orbit spitting on the stars in the pavement. Every man and woman... huh.

Strange over the top drugged hyper-acting hate comic on TV – homophobic, racist (?), suss, bad time with women – hates 'em, hellish marriage you can tell – very disturbing – fat, raincoat, drop down dead in a heatwave vibes, very honest, very funny because so into reality – his own – touches on the very personal – anyone with tragic moments of any variety – relationships etc – will form at least a small empathetic link with this guy – therefore his genius is he knows how to tap into the universal and objective mixed with the no longer hidden subjective – perfect – more so because controversial – the smart loser; you can see it though, the evil in there, the hurt, the black vile/bile at his core. This guy is dangerous (to himself). [This turned out to be Sam Kinison (1953-92), stand-up and actor].

Sitting on the Astro roof garden writing/Disturbed by X, G and M/X wants to see what I'm writing/I refuse/Later she reads it anyway. The problem with her is always one of secrecy and openness. I stop writing.

Diary ends.

TITLE
Ripped Backsides – The Passenger, from *Lust for Life* (1977),
Iggy Pop; also from an unnamed poem by Jim Morrison.

Postcards from Beneath the Pavement – slogan popular during
the 1968 protests in France: 'Sous les pavés, la plage!' ('Beneath
the pavement, the beach').

AMSTERDAM (1984)
Walter Benjamin's image is *detached from aura by mechanical
reproduction*. But what about dramatic tension? – *The Work
of Art in the Age of Mechanical Reproduction*, (1935), Walter
Benjamin.

Dialogue: Godard says the real problem is to get back to zero –
agreed? – *Joy of Learning* (French: Le Gai savoir) (1969), film
by Jean-Luc Godard.

**BARCELONA, VALENCIA and MADRID (1968, 2004
and several assorted years over the 1980s, 1990s and 2000s)**
Art and symmetry provide respite. But just for a short while.
Scratch in the sand, won't let go his hand. – The Jean Genie
(1972), David Bowie.

People say quoting some book they have read on the bus: 'I
never get nowhere but I pay my own fare all the way.' Better
to just walk. – *The Man with the Golden Arm* (1949), Nelson
Algren.

People read Keats about those who pass into nothingness ... –
Sleep and Poetry (1816) *Endymion* (1818) *When I Have Fears*
(1818), John Keats.

BERLIN (1987)
Avoid at all costs: Temporary autonomous zones. – *T.A.Z.:
The Temporary Autonomous Zone* (1991), Hakim Bey

LONDON (1978-present)
I believe in rampant ambition, in books that start with people
who are afraid to merge on freeways in Los Angeles – *Less than
Zero* (1987), Bret Easton Ellis.

... in Bryon Gysin's assertion that: *no, poets don't own words,*

– No Poets Don't Own Words, from *Brion Gysin's Recordings 1960-1981*, Brion Gysin.

... in Godard's remark that tracking shots are a question of ethics – From a 1959 round-table discussion of *Hiroshima mon Amour* (Alain Resnais, 1959).

... in Lou Reed's idea that electricity comes from other planets –*Temptation Inside your Heart* (1968/1984), The Velvet Underground.

I believe in having hair swept backwards and aloft as if caught in a sudden gust, in looking for a kiss, in *Looking for a Kiss – Richard Cabut on Creative Divination, Existential Vertigo, and His New Book of Poetry, Disorderly Magic & Other Disturbances*, in *Write or Die*, Lydia Sviatoslavsky (2023).

Life is photography, death is cinema – Susan Sontag upside down, spinning over and over, once more, in her grave. – *The Benefactor* (1963), Susan Sontag.

MANCHESTER (1985, 2020, 2022, 2023, 2024)
Fiction romance – a personal myth, therefore absolute and true – *Fiction Romance*, (1978), Buzzcocks.

MARSEILLES (2019)
Jim Morrison, the city trembles over any activity that appears to have no meaning – Jim Morrison interviewed in *Rolling Stone* (1969).

Metaphysical suicide, says Sartre, smoking. – *Being and Nothingness: An Essay on Phenomenological Ontology* (1943), Jean-Paul Sartre.

NEW YORK (1989, 2023, 2024)
City says real life is just performance art. Like Arthur Rimbaud in New York. – *Arthur Rimbaud in New York* (1978 and 1980), David Wojnarowicz.

People in clubs go home to flush away the drugs in their coats. But suddenly remember there are No More Coats and No More Home. – *The Revolution of Everyday Life* (1967), Raoul Vaneigem.

The glass moves on its own. – *Stalker* (1979), Andrei Tarkovsky.

... baffling smoke signals, like Lee Perry – *Baffling Smoke Signal* (1978), Lee Perry.

Negative Girl says city is accidental. – *Negative Girls* (1982), Victor Bockris.

Charles Bukowski says he isn't sure whether *it's good poetry or bad acid.* – *Love Is a Dog from Hell* (1977), Charles Bukowski.

... it's a play about the rehearsal of a play. – *The Rehearsal* (1672), Anonymous, ('but it is certainly by George Villiers, 2nd Duke of Buckingham and others').

PARIS, ST ETIENNE, LILLE, BORDEAUX (1972, 2006, 2011, 2021 etc – several visits over the 80s, 90s, etc)
Good taste is death, vulgarity is life. People have taken Mary Quant's sentiment to heart. – Mary Quant interviewed in the *Guardian* (1967).

Patti Smith the city seeks *the nerves under your skin.* – *Babelogue/Rock 'n' Roll Nigger* (1978), from *Easter*, Patti Smith.

ROME, NAPLES, LECCE, ANZIO, THE AMALFI COAST (1990, 2021, etc)
Woman on metro looking for: Brand new revenge. – Song by the band Max, 1986.

Dialogue: Tell your sister I'll throw bricks with her. – Song by the band Max, 1986.

WARSAW and KRAKOW (1967, 2077, 2022, etc)
'Couple face one another holding inside hands (man R girl L), free hand extended, etc' –
A Selection of European Folk Dances: Volume 1, (1956), Sam Stuart.

APPENDIX – CREATIVE DIRECTORY / TAXONOMY (EXCERPTS) – NEW YORK (EAST VILLAGE/WEST VILLAGE/BUSHWICK), (July 1989 and April 2023)
Question: Do you know how to Pony? – *Land: Horses/ Land of a Thousand Dances / La Mer (De)*, from *Horses* (1975), Patti Smith.

People quote Dante all the time: *Predestined turning point of God's intention.* – *The Divine Comedy* (1321), Dante.

In no particular order.

The Ruined Map – Kobo Abe
The Peasants – Wladyslaw Reymont
Book of Disquiet – Fernando Pessoa
A Short History of Decay – EM Cioran
The Drowned World – JG Ballard
Metamorphoses – Ovid
Ubik – Philip K Dick
Where the Stress Falls – Susan Sontag
Andrei Tarkovsky: The Screenplays – Andrei Tarkovsky
The Game of War: The Life and Death of Guy Debord, and *Paris*
– Andrew Hussey
Almost Transparent Blue – Ryu Murakami
Less than Zero – Bret Easton Ellis
Infinite Resignation – Eugene Thacker
Revolt, She Said – Julia Kristeva
Godard: Images, Sounds, Politics – Colin MacCabe
In the Dark Room – Brian Dillon
The Philosophy of Andy Warhol: from A to B and Back Again –
Andy Warhol
A Year with Swollen Appendices: Brian Eno's Diary – Brian Eno
The Tightrope Walker – Hermine Demoriane
Magical Record of the Beast 666 – Aleister Crowley
Reeling – Pauline Kael
House of the Angels – Timothy Wilson
Meetings with Remarkable Men: All and Everything – George
I Gurdjieff
Big Sur – Jack Kerouac
*The Ring of Brightest Angels Around Heaven: A Novella and
Stories* – Rick Moody
Generation X: Tales for an Accelerated Culture – Douglas
Coupland
Complete Cinematic Works – Guy Debord
Slow Days, Fast Company: The World, the Flesh, and LA – Eve
Babitz
Disaster was my God – Bruce Duffy
The Flowers of Evil – Charles Baudelaire
*From Manchester with Love: The Life and Opinions of Tony
Wilson* – Paul Morley

AUTHOR

Richard Cabut is author of the novel *Looking for a Kiss* (PC-Press, 2023).

A Freudian 80s post-punk fairy tale – *bad weather in the English soul.*

The book has been adapted for the screen.

And of the number one poetry/modern literature book *Disorderly Magic and Other Disturbances* (Far West Press, 2023).

The work mixes magic, culture, mystery, memoir, history, melodrama – it is an invocation, an evocation, with dreamlike freedom of movement between past and present, from personal to universal.

Also, the novel *Dark Entries* (Cold Lips Press, 2019).

JOURNALIST

Richard's journalism has featured in the *Guardian*, the *Daily Telegraph*, *NME* (pen name Richard North), *ZigZag*, *The Big Issue*, *Time Out*, *Offbeat* magazine, the *Independent*, *Artists & Illustrators* magazine, *thefirstpost*, London Arts Board/ Arts Council England, *Siren* magazine, etc. He was a Features Writer with the BBC for several years.

WRITER

He co-edited/-contributed to the anthology *Punk is Dead: Modernity Killed Every Night* (Zer0 Books, October 2017), and was also a contributor to *Ripped, Torn and Cut – Pop, Politics and Punks Fanzines From 1976* (Manchester University Press, 2018) and *Growing Up With Punk* (Nice Time, 2018).

His short fiction has appeared in the books *Pretty Obscure* (Far West Press, 2024), *The Edgier Waters* (Snowbooks, 2006) and *Affinity* (67 Press, 2015).

He was a Pushcart Prize nominee 2016.

His poetry has appeared in *An Anthology of Punk Ass Poetry* (Orchid Eater Press, 2022), and cult magazines such as *3ammagazine*, etc.

He published the fanzine *Kick* (1979-82).

Richard's plays have been performed at various theatres in London and nationwide, including the Arts Theatre, Covent Garden, London.

MUSICIAN

He played bass for the band Brigandage (LP *Pretty Funny Thing* – Gung Ho Records, 1986). And co-wrote/performed the track *Unkempt Magic* on the LP *Dark Jazz* by The Necessary Animals (2022)

ACADEMIC

Visiting Lecturer Contextual Studies (design and theory), University of East London.

FILM

Short film *Flux Dreams Awake* selected for and shown at Fourth World Congress of Psychogeography, Canterbury Christ Church University. September, 2024. With Simon Beesley.

https://en.wikipedia.org/wiki/Richard_Cabut

richardcabut.com

ACKNOWLEDGEMENTS AND CREDITS

Heartfelt thanks to: Willie Crane, Jeff Young, Lyss Lester, Sylvie Selig, Margaret Arana, Laura Board, Bernie and Aniela Cabut, Lydia Sviatoslavsky, and Leighanne Murray

This book was written largely to the accompaniment of the radio shows: *On the Wire, Outernational Sounds*, etc

ALSO OUT ON FAR WEST

farwestpress.com
+1 (541) FAR-WEST